DEADLY MEMORY

LIVING MEMORY SERIES
BOOK 2

DAVID WALTON

CONTENTS

for Silas
fellow fantastical story creator

CHAPTER ONE

San Julian Basin, off the coast of Argentina

D r. Elena Benitez was obsessed with extinction.

Her obsession had brought her here, to the deck of the *Storm Petrel* drilling rig in the South Atlantic, a hundred kilometers from the nearest coastline. She could see nothing but endless blue water in every direction. A gust of wind ruffled her hair and brought the smell of salt and seaweed. Despite the biting cold, she smiled. She had chased this dream for her whole life, it seemed, and now, finally, she was almost there.

Her preoccupation with extinction had begun as a young graduate student, when the last few Titicaca water frogs in the world had died under her care. The perpetrator of this amphibian genocide had been a fungus that grew on the skins of the unfortunate frogs and toads who caught it. Starting in Asia over a century earlier, it had spread around the world through the live animal trade and killed off eighty-five percent of the world's amphibian species. It was the worst infectious disease in recorded history, and most people had never even heard of it.

Extinction, it turned out, was nearly as common as life. Everyone knew about the famous asteroid strike that had killed the dinosaurs, but there had been other great extinctions, too, some of them even more destructive. Elena's professional curiosity had gradually focused on the end-Permian extinction, which had occurred *before* the dinosaurs, clearing out the previous large land animals to make room for the dinos to grow and thrive. The Permian extinction was known as The Great Dying, and it had been the greatest of all extinction events, killing ninety percent of the species on the planet. It had come perilously close to eradicating life entirely.

The most intriguing part for her as a scientist was this: no one knew why. You could walk along an exposed shelf of Permian rock and see fossil remains of all kinds of animals: lizards with sails on their backs, reptiles with huge tusks, spiny fish, and the ubiquitous trilobites, twenty thousand species strong. Cross the line of the extinction event, and they all disappeared. An empty zone at the beginning of the Triassic, with almost no fossils at all.

What had happened? Like an Agatha Christie murder mystery, there were many suspects but no clear perpetrator. Had it been another asteroid? Massive volcanic eruptions? Acid rain? Microbes that converted oxygen into methane? Theories abounded, but there was no smoking gun.

Like Walter Alvarez, who discovered the asteroid that ended the dinosaurs, Elena wanted to be the detective who finally solved the Permian extinction mystery for certain. That obsession was what had sent her, finally, out to sea on this aging drillship to a place where surveys showed a thick layer of Permian rock under the seabed.

The metal platform belched and clanked under her as drill engineers worked to replace a used drill bit. They had been drilling into the ocean floor for days now. The goal was to retrieve core samples—long cylinders of rock cut deep into the Earth's crust—which could then be analyzed back in the lab, layer by layer. Core samples of this sort had been taken many times before around the globe, but the survey data for this location had shown several unique characteristics that Elena was looking for.

She ducked out of the wind and descended to the moon pool, a sheltered area beneath the derrick that allowed direct access to the water. The engineers were lowering the pipe with another fresh drill bit into the water. Each time a drill bit wore out, they had to pull up the entire pipe, change the bit, and then thread the pipe back down into the hole at the bottom of the ocean, a difficult and sophisticated procedure involving sonar scanning and precision instrumentation.

Once the pipe was in place, Elena and her team watched indoors on a screen that showed the drill's depth overlaid with survey data. As it churned its way through Triassic limestone and into the sedimentary rock of the Permian era, they cheered. They still had days of drilling to go to reach the bottom of the layer, but it was an occasion worth celebrating.

A burst of chimes from Elena's phone announced incoming text messages. Even with their signal boosters, cell coverage was rare out here, but every once in a while, the stars aligned, and she would get a brief connection, enough to deliver her missed messages.

The texts were from her daughter, Gabriela, who was currently on a dig in Thailand with Samira Shannon. Elena was glad Gabby had found a good team and was establishing her career. Apparently, they'd uncovered a new theropod species. *They're kicking us out of the country*, her text said. Elena frowned. Thailand had always been open to foreign scientists.

Shouts of alarm from outside interrupted her. Elena dropped the phone on the table, leaving the rest of the message unread, and clanged up the metal stairs to the platform. Black mud geysered from the open pipe, spattering the drill derrick and the deck. Engineers ran for cover. The water in the moon pool bubbled and spat.

"Capture it!" Elena shouted. "We need uncontaminated samples!"

She snatched a plastic bin used to store lengths of core and held it next to the pipe, capturing mud as it frothed over the edge. Her hands were quickly covered in muck, and black spatter decorated her shirt, face, and hair. As the flow sputtered and finally stopped, Elena stood, triumphant, wiping 250-million-year-old filth on her jeans. It had to be pulverized rock mixed with water and probably some kind of gas, maybe hydrogen, to make it bubble like that. It was completely unexpected, and unexpected results meant new knowledge. By the end of the week, she was sure, they would know more about the Permian extinction than they knew now.

It took less than a day before people began to get sick. No one connected it to the mud. Why would they? Disease was conveyed by living organisms, after all. Pulverized rock only caused sickness if you breathed the dust or it was radioactive. And rock drilled from deep under the ocean floor couldn't possibly have microbes in it.

Like everyone else, Elena assumed someone on the team had boarded already infected with a virus and had then spread it to others in the confined quarters. It wasn't severe; just a mild cough. Nothing to worry about.

By the time they reached shore, almost everyone had it, but no one even bothered to see a doctor. They kissed their spouses, visited relatives, interacted with waitresses, cashiers, and friends. The sickness spread.

Two days later, one of the drill engineers collapsed suddenly on the street, spasming and drowning in his own saliva and vomit. His wife said he'd been fine moments before. Before the day was out, five more people died similarly, including two of Elena's colleagues. By that time, dozens more had been infected.

Elena never did get to study the sample of mud she'd brought back in its plastic bin, and neither did anyone on her team. She never even realized the mud and the sickness were connected.

Elena's career ended as it began. With extinction.

CHAPTER TWO

The first thing Prey smelled was himself. He reeked. He rarely went even a few hours without a bath, and judging by the odor, it had been days at least. He hoped no one else was around. As far as he could smell, though, no one was nearby, not for miles.

He sifted the air through his nostrils. Strange. No one at all. He couldn't smell the city network, or any of the rural nodes, or...anything. No plants, no earth, no rain, no life at all. The oxygen content of the air was low, with a taste of carbon dioxide and a lot more nitrogen than he was used to. Where was he?

He opened his eyes. He was in a cave. That explained some of it, though there was no smell of damp or mold or feces. Five weird-looking animals stood in the mouth of the cave. They stood upright and had flat, soft, hairless faces, except for one with fur on its jaws. They were tall, but with no hide, no armor, no claws, and tiny teeth. No threat, in other words.

But he couldn't smell them, either, which terrified him. Had he lost his sense of smell? But no, he could still smell his own rank body odor. How could these creatures be alive, but have no scent at all?

They opened their mouths and moved their tongues as if making a noise, but no noise came out. If he'd been hungry, he might have killed one to see what it tasted like. Stupid creatures didn't even know to run away from a predator. He flew at them, claws out and teeth bared, to scatter them...and slammed headlong into something hard. Pain lanced through his face and neck, flooding him with adrenaline and fury. He lashed out blindly, expecting an attack, but found nothing. When he looked, the creatures hadn't moved. They opened their mouths and seemed more alert, but didn't run. They just looked at each other and continued to move their tongues with no sound.

His head rang from the impact, and he felt dizzy. What had he run into? He reached out tentatively and felt an invisible barrier. He tapped it. Hard, like stone. Now that he knew it was there, he could see it, barely. Light glared off its surface in places, and he could see his own reflection faintly, as if in water. What was it? Some kind of new technology? A surface made out of frozen air?

He followed the surface with his eyes, saw how transparent panels slotted into a frame of a hard, shiny substance. Now that he looked, he saw that the rest of the cave was formed from the same shiny substance, and stood in perfectly smooth, vertical walls. Not just approximately vertical, but carved vertical with a precision he had never seen before. Above and below him, the same substance penned him in.

This wasn't a cave. It was a prison.

He tried to remember what he had done to get here, but it was all a blur. Had he been captured by another roost? The wall of frozen air not only blocked him from escaping, but blocked scent and sound as well. Whoever had done this, they had isolated him from the rest of civilization so he couldn't send for help or transmit his location. He didn't know such complete isolation was possible, but obviously it was.

The animals on the other side of the barrier apparently knew he couldn't reach them, which was why they showed no fear. Despite their exotic appearance, they were probably domesticated animals kept for food. Did that mean he was in a distant roost, with unfamiliar food and customs? Were these creatures meant to be fed to him? Perhaps at some point the invisible barrier would be lowered, allowing him to reach them and eat.

He couldn't remember being captured or how it had happened. But why him? He was nothing. He was just a...a...

Terror gripped him again as he tried to remember. He didn't know his name. He couldn't bring his own scent marker to mind. How was that possible? What had they done to him?

A scraping sound caught his attention, and he turned. A hole had opened in one wall. *Smells* came through the hole, a rich rush of them, some familiar and others alien. Even though he knew his captors wanted him to, he couldn't help it —he ducked through the hole to see what was on the other side.

He found himself in a cage formed from bars of the same hard, shiny substance. This one, however, was open to the air. More of the strange animals stood on the other side of the cage, watching him. He could smell them now, warm meat and blood. He could smell other things on them too—traces of plants and oils and other unidentifiable things. He had thought their soft outer coverings were part of their bodies, but now he realized they were artificial coverings made from plant matter. Several of the animals had strong, complex odors, as if they had been tagged, though if they had, it wasn't in any language he could understand.

One of the animals reached out its small, curiously weak hands and pulled a lever. With a grinding noise, a hook lowered from above. A large slab of meat hung from the hook, dripping blood on the floor. When it came within reach, the grinding noise stopped.

It smelled at least three hours dead. His stomach gurgled, but he had no intention of eating meat that someone else had killed, as if he were an infant. Was it meant to be an insult? Show him fresh prey and then feed him old meat?

Everything about this situation was wrong. Where were his captors? If the panels of frozen air were meant to block scent, why did they let him out into an enclosure that didn't block it at all? He couldn't smell anyone other than himself—not a trace, as if no one had ever entered this cave at all.

An explanation had been forming in the back of his mind for some time, but until now he had pushed it aside. He stared at the creatures through the bars, taking in their focused gaze, their fluid interaction with the objects around them, the precise fit of the plant matter coverings to their bodies. He considered all the unfamiliar material and technology, and the fact that it had been one of the *animals* that had pulled the lever that lowered the meat. He had always prided himself on his ability to see things as they were instead of how he wanted them to be. To face the facts and act accordingly.

Was it possible? They were so clearly prey, soft and vulnerable. But as hard as it was to accept, it seemed that *they* were his captors. An alien species, an *intelligent* species, with technology beyond his imagination.

A flash of memory came back to him, more emotion than detail. The coming cataclysm, predicted but unavoidable. The authority of the roosts, falling apart. Panic and infighting. A chance to save a few, to preserve them far into the future, beyond the effect of the cataclysm, where they could start again.

It was then that he truly began to be afraid.

And he still couldn't remember his name.

CHAPTER THREE

S amira stared at the dinosaur, barely able to process what she was seeing.

The creature stretched and shook its feathered neck, sending tufts of brown fluff drifting to the concrete floor. It stood around five feet tall, its limbs covered with filamentous protofeathers, and looked for all the world like a giant bird. Its jaw resembled a beak except for the sharp teeth inside, and its huge nostrils had no septum, like a vulture's, providing a direct opening to sinuses so big you could see straight through from one side to the other. It preened briefly, and she caught sight of one hand, complete with double opposable thumbs.

Beth touched her shoulder through the hazmat suit, and the two of them shared a look of utter wonder.

"Incredible," Beth said.

Samira remembered to breathe. "It's not possible." She turned to Paula. "You can't have done this. DNA never lasts this long."

"Never say never," Paula said, her smile mischievous. She was clearly enjoying this. Even Dan Everson, who she didn't think had cracked a smile since the day he showed up at her doorstep to interrogate her about Thailand, seemed delighted at their astonishment.

"It's impossible," Samira insisted, as the impossible thing stared back at her from behind the glass. "How?"

Paula turned serious. "You're right. We can't do it. *They* did it." She pointed to the creature in the cage. "They preserved themselves. They saw the extinction event coming and tried to survive it."

"So...the dig site..."

"One of several hibernation chambers. I don't know how many there were. The Chinese found the first one."

"You knew all along," Beth said. "Before we even left for Thailand, you knew."

"She was bound by law not to reveal what she knew," Everson said. "As, I may add, are the two of you."

Paula had the grace to look embarrassed. "I didn't know as much as you think. We had a few fossils, some reports of the chemical and what it could do. This facility was built long before we put it to this use. So yes, I may have nudged your team in the right direction and directed some funding your way, but I had no idea the monumental nature of what you would discover."

Samira shook her head, not getting it. "This maniraptor is full-grown, or close to it," she said. "That's five years you've been here, minimum."

"You don't understand," Paula said. "This isn't like Lewis the dodo or George Church's baby mammoth. Charlie wasn't born from a specially-fertilized ostrich egg. We didn't harvest DNA and use it to create a viable ovum. Charlie was there in the ground all the time. Once we understood what we had, it took all our scientific knowledge and some we hadn't invented yet to revive him. But ultimately, it wasn't our technology that did it. It was theirs."

Samira felt lightheaded. She reached for a wall to steady herself. "You're telling me that the creature in there is what we brought back from Thailand? That *this specific maniraptor* was alive in the Cretaceous period? And you brought him back to life?"

"Technically, he never died. The technology that preserved him goes well beyond cryogenics. It preserves soft tissue, cell membranes, nerves. As far as we can figure, they intended to wake themselves in a relatively short time, ten or twenty or a hundred years, once the worst of the devastation had passed. Instead, they never woke, and most of them died when geological shifts broke open their hibernation chambers."

"The memories you experienced in Thailand, when you inhaled that chemical," Beth said.

"Yes," Paula said. "Those were real, as far as we can tell. They actually happened, sixty-six million years ago. Of the thousands that went into hibernation, only this one made it through all the changes to its environment over the eons. Even so, he almost died. The first few hours after he came out of hibernation were touch and go."

"So for the entire history of mankind, it's been underground," Samira said, still trying to process it. If the dinosaur itself wasn't standing in front of her, she probably wouldn't have believed it at all.

"Yes."

"And it was there. For the asteroid collision. It remembers it happening."

"He may even be the one who realized it was coming. We can't be sure that the memory you described connects to this individual, but if so, he was the one who mobilized a mass hibernation in an attempt to outlive it."

"And you call him Charlie?" Beth asked.

Paula laughed. "We had to call him something."

"If the memories I experienced were his," Samira said, "then his name was something more like 'recently killed prey.'

Though it was a smell associated with a concept, not a spoken word."

Paula made a face. "We can't exactly call him that, can we?"

Samira started to pace. Now that her shock was wearing off, the anger was building. "I can't believe you've been keeping this from us."

Paula's voice grew somber. "Samira."

"You've been sitting on this miracle all this time. It's been almost six months, and nobody even returned my phone calls. How could you do this to us?"

"I wanted to tell you."

"No! I don't understand you. Why is this a secret at all? Why are you working with the *government*? You're a scientist. We don't hide things. We don't bury discoveries in giant underground vaults and lock the world out. How can we make progress if we don't share results?"

"You're upset."

Samira took a breath. This was Paula, not some government bureaucrat. "I'm sorry. But yes, I am upset. You let Beth and me go off to Thailand, knowing all this, and you didn't tell us anything. We didn't know what we were looking at, because we didn't have all the information. We spent months on that dig, and they took everything we found. If we had only known—"

"You would have what? Fought the Thai government? You did everything you could."

Samira stopped pacing and looked her former mentor in the eyes. "Why is this a secret, Paula? Why aren't we telling the world?"

"You're about to see why."

"See? What do you mean?"

"You're in luck," Paula said. "It's feeding time."

THE WHITE-TAILED DEER reluctantly walked through the open gate into the larger cage, prodded from behind by a hazmat-suited handler with a long staff. The doe had never seen the kind of creature that awaited it inside, but it quaked all the same.

The maniraptor made no move.

"Watch what happens," Paula said.

The doe pranced nervously, its hooves clacking on the concrete floor. It reversed direction, trying to go back the way it had come, but the handler had already shut the gate. Its nostrils flared. Then it relaxed.

"Here it comes," Paula said.

The deer walked at a calm, steady pace toward the maniraptor. It lifted its head high, exposing the thick arteries of its neck. The maniraptor, unhurried, opened its mouth and rested its teeth on the deer's throat. The deer just stood there, visibly trembling, its eyes rolling back in its head, but it made no move to get away. In a swift motion, the maniraptor clamped its jaws shut and tore away a huge chunk of flesh, fountaining blood across the concrete of the floor and the glass window. The deer collapsed to the ground.

Samira shook her head, amazed. "So that's where it comes from."

"You've seen this before?" Paula asked.

Samira looked at Beth. "Worse. I've experienced it. We both have."

"This is why you're wearing a hazmat suit," Paula said. "This is why no one ever comes in here without one. Charlie can produce pheromones that dominate other creatures, forcing them into submission. Dominating them even to the extent that—as you just saw—they willingly collaborate in their own deaths."

"I thought pheromones only worked within a single species, to mark territory or attract mates," Beth said.

"Most do. Others are used to lull prey into a false sense of security, or to confuse predators. The arms race can get somewhat complicated, as predators and prey evolve to respond to each other's chemical signals. These maniraptors have something extraordinary, though. We think it must have evolved in tandem with their sense of smell, which is off the charts. Charlie here can smell better than any living animal today. And considering the incredible smelling abilities some living animals have, that's saying something.

"He has scent glands all over his body—on his face, between his claws, on his neck. At our best estimate, he can produce over ten thousand different odors, as well as complex combinations of those odors."

"So, apple pie, then?" Samira said. "Freshly baked bread?"

"Chamomile tea would be my pick," Paula said. "And I'm sure he could, if he wanted to. It's their primary sense, more than vision, more than hearing. It probably developed originally as a way to enforce the pecking order, to communicate dominance and force submission within the tribe. These creatures had a language, but it wasn't a vocal one. They don't hear very well, and they don't have much vocal variety. Their principal communication medium was through their sense of smell."

"You seem pretty sure of that."

Paula smiled enigmatically. "More on that later. There's only so much we can cover on day one."

Samira watched Charlie tear bloody strips of meat from the deer's carcass, letting Paula's explanation sink in. The feathers near his mouth were stained red. "So you think he's intelligent enough to have a language. A true general language like ours, not like Marcy, where it's all warnings about danger and directions to where the food is."

"Oh, he's far smarter than a raven," Paula said. "We have to stay on our toes around here. We put him to sleep sometimes so we can clean his cage or study him more closely. One time he faked sleep after we pumped the gas in, and Alex, one of our handlers, went in too soon. Charlie flicked out a claw and tore the hazmat suit. Didn't touch his body and didn't attack. Not everyone agrees, but I think Charlie understands that we're intelligent and understands that the suits are clothes, not part of our body. He didn't want to hurt Alex; he just wanted to smell him."

"What happened to Alex?" Samira asked.

"He was fine. Scared half to death, and he had to stay in quarantine for a week to make sure, but yeah. We're more careful now."

"So if he has a language," Beth said, "Have you tried to learn it?"

Paula chuckled. "It would be hard enough learning a brand-new spoken language. But one composed of smells? No."

"So what, you haven't even tried? No linguists on staff?" Samira asked.

"We've had other priorities."

Samira thought about that. "You mean your bosses have other priorities, don't you? The government doesn't care about paleontology or learning about an ancient civilization. They want their secret chemical weapon that can make people do whatever they want."

"Yes, that's true," Paula admitted. "That is what they care about, and they're paying the bills. But Samira, it *has* to be a secret. Think of what it means if that chemical gets out into the world. Think about date rape and kidnapping and drug cults. Think of all the evil that could be done with such a power."

"No," Samira said. "Paula, this is terrible! How can you support this?" She thought of the papers she had so willingly signed, agreeing to prosecution or imprisonment if she revealed what she learned. "If it's out in the open, then we can regulate it, control its use."

"Like we do with cocaine and heroin?" Paula asked. "Not a great track record there."

"So you want the CIA to have it? Or the military? So they can drop a cloud of it on some foreign town before the troops march in?"

Paula sighed. "You would rather the Chinese got there first?"

Samira turned away, furious with her, and furious with herself for walking into this. She did not want to be a party to chemical weapons manufacture. "So those people up on the eighth floor, drilling holes in black market fossils. Is this what they're extracting?"

"They get a little bit that way, but not much. Most of it comes from Charlie himself."

She turned back. "From Charlie?"

"From his scent glands. Twice a day, we put him to sleep and extract chemicals from scent glands on the sides of his neck."

"So you're in the business of extracting drugs from live animals now?"

Paula put a hand on her arm. "I think you're getting the wrong impression. This is a scientific operation, despite the security. There's no pressure to develop military applications. I actually set a lot of the research goals myself. Yes, there are military concerns, but give it a chance. Get to know the people here. There's so much to learn! Not just about the pheromones, but all the rest, too—how did their hibernation chambers work? How could they possibly preserve life for all that time? Organic structures just don't survive that long; they break down. Think about it, Samira: for the first time ever, we have an *actual, living dinosaur* to study! There's so much new we're discovering, so much we're reevaluating that we thought we knew before."

"And publishing your findings?" Samira asked. "Sharing your discoveries with the rest of the scientific community?"

Paula's face fell. "Eventually, I hope. You have to under-stand, it's this or nothing. The government isn't going to let this go public, not when there's so much at stake with the Chinese. You can like it or you can hate it, but that's the world we live in. These are serious people, and you don't want to cross them. On the other hand, they've given us everything we've asked for to pursue our own goals, without regard to whether it's directly profitable to them. You can walk away, but please, Samira. Stay. There's so much work to do."

Samira turned to look at the creature on the other side of the glass. Charlie looked back at her alertly, his dark eyes intent.

Study the find of the century, or walk away? It wasn't a question, not really. She felt like she was letting her conscience slip away a layer at a time, but how could she know this was here and not be a part of it?

She looked at Beth, who had stood there quietly through most of the conversation. "What do you think?"

Beth took her hand through the hazmat suit. Her eyes were shining, her face full of awe. "It's a *dinosaur*," she said.

Samira sighed. "I won't regret this a year from now, will I?"

"Not a chance," Paula said.

CHAPTER FOUR

The creatures in their smell-proof suits moved around outside the cage. There were two new ones with them today. Their suits blocked most smells, but since they touched the outside of the suits when they put them on, he could still identify each of them by what they left behind.

They put a food animal in his cage. At least they gave him live meat now. The animal stared at Prey, motionless except for the rise and fall of its chest. It stood on four thin and brittle legs with hard tips instead of feet, and its body was covered in soft brown fur except for a splash of white on its tail. They had given him this kind of animal before, but Prey watched it carefully, ignoring his grumbling stomach until he was sure it posed no threat.

Eventually, he could wait no longer. He generated a scent to dominate the creature. Its legs tensed as if it would spring, but after an initial moment of terror, it calmed. At his instruction, it walked meekly over to him and stretched out its neck. He buried his jaws in its throat. Warm blood pulsed into his mouth. The creature twitched and went still.

Prey took his time, tearing off strips of raw flesh and

chewing them slowly. His nostrils filled with the scent of the kill, but he could still smell his captors. They spent a lot of their time just watching him. Sometimes they put objects in his cage. Sometimes they pumped an odorless air into the cage that made him go to sleep. He had no idea what they did to him then, but often he woke with a raw ache in the glands on his neck.

Over time, Prey had remembered his name, the asteroid, and the panicked emotions of those final days, but the details still eluded him. He could remember descending into the modification pit, expecting to die, but hoping to emerge again a few months later, after the worst of the damage had passed. What had happened since then? Was the sun still blocked by debris? How many had survived?

He had tried to escape his prison once. He had gripped the mesh with his fingers and hurled his powerful rear legs at it, cutting into the thick strands with his claws. The result had been a flash and a paralyzing blast of horrific pain, like what he imagined it would be like to be struck by lightning. Had these creatures harnessed lightning? Could they strike with it at will?

Prey had decided then to be patient. He knew almost nothing of these creatures or his surroundings. Escape would mean little if he had nowhere to escape to. He needed to wait, to learn, to find out as much as he could about them without revealing too much of himself.

They didn't seem to want to communicate. The transparent barrier and their suits blocked most chemical transfer. He couldn't tell what they wanted or even attempt to share his desires or ask questions. Their suits must also block any chemical transfer between themselves, too, which was strange. He could understand isolating him, but why did they isolate each other?

Unless they didn't exchange chemical information at all. Was that possible? They seemed to vocalize a lot, judging by how much they moved their mouths and throats. Whenever they did, noises came out of a mesh box mounted high in his cage. He assumed it must be the noises their mouths made—the correlation was undeniable—but how did they throw the sound like that? It was like speaking into a long hollow tube and having the sound come out the other side, but there was no hollow tube between their suits and the top of his cage.

He found it hard to believe that a species could develop this level of coordinated activity and invention without direct chemical communication. Vocalizations just didn't convey enough information. Worse, sounds were transient, disappearing almost immediately with no way to record the data. Unless these creatures had amazing memories, most of their ideas would be lost. How could they develop an advanced civilization without being able to capture their thoughts and pass them on to future generations?

There had to be more to it. Maybe they communicated directly through thought, or by some other mechanism he'd never even imagined. There was so much he didn't understand. Until he could find a way to communicate—or escape—he had no way to answer the questions burning through his brain. He had to be patient. He wanted them to think he was harmless, or at least completely under their control. The more docile they thought he was, the more they would let their guard down. He could wait. Eventually, they would make a mistake.

CHAPTER FIVE

K it didn't know the American was there until he walked into the throne room and saw him.

Princess Sirindhorn sat on the dais at the front. Despite the fact that she held court in the lobby of a Marriott hotel in Chiang Rai, not in the palace in Bangkok, she was resplendent. She wore a fuchsia dress in military cut, with a white sash and medals pinned to her chest and her hair piled high. Her bodyguards, who called themselves the Daughters of the Queen, stood on either side, every one of them women rescued from slavery. They might not be as well-trained as professional guards, but they were fiercely loyal and willing to die for her.

Kit stood for a moment and stared at her, in awe as always. Mai. He still wasn't used to referring to her by her personal nickname. He could barely believe he was allowed to talk to her at all. As her science minister, however, he was now one of her few trusted advisors, privy to all her plans and affairs.

Which is why he was startled to find her speaking with an American CIA agent, a meeting he was unaware had been taking place. He stepped across the room and quietly took his place on the raised platform, next to Arinya Tavaranan.

"What's going on?" he whispered to Arinya.

She glared at him. "Shh. Just listen."

"Your Grace," the American said. "Wattana's corrupt government is weakening Thailand. We would see Thailand strong."

"Strong and dancing to an American tune?" Mai asked.

The American shook his head. He was muscular beneath his suit, and far too handsome, like a Hollywood movie star. "We want the same things you do," he said smoothly. "A free and independent Thailand. A Thailand strong enough not to be bullied and manipulated by China. We both know Wattana is a fraud and a puppet. You are not only the country's rightful ruler, but also the leader Thailand needs. The United States does not want to interfere with your revolution. We just want to help."

"And what help are you prepared to offer?" Mai asked.

"Guns," the American said. "Intelligence. Communications technology. The capability to know where your adversaries are at all times and what they are saying to each other."

Mai's serene expression gave nothing away. "And what do you ask in return?"

The American spread his hands. "China is becoming too powerful. We don't want to see Thailand become just a province of the PRC. With you on the throne, that will not happen. That is all we want."

"No," Kit said. It came out louder than he intended, resounding in the echoing space. Heads swiveled toward him in surprise. He knew he should leave this to Mai, but he felt too angry to stop. "We are not an American tool," he said. "We are not a shield you can use to block Chinese expansion without dirtying your own hands. We will not fight your proxy war. You want us to keep the snake out of our house by inviting in the scorpion! Thailand does not belong to China, but neither does it belong to the United States. We will fight our own battles, and we will rule our own country."

The American took a step back and bowed his head slightly, but he continued to address Mai, not Kit. "Believe me, your Majesty, that is what we want as well. We offer you services only. No strings. No hidden costs. We simply want you to succeed."

But Kit wasn't done. "And when we are dependent on the drug of American aid? When our ability to hold power is inextricably linked to the services you provide? You talk a good game, *farang*, but your gifts are poisoned. Her Majesty's family was ruling Thailand when you were still a handful of colonies shaking your fists at the British. She needs no help from you."

The American kept his gaze on Mai, waiting.

"You heard my minister," she said calmly. "Thailand appreciates our long friendship with our American allies. We seek to continue that relationship throughout our reign. We are grateful for the help you offer and the spirit of cooperation it implies. However, we have no need for aid."

The American looked astonished. Kit wondered if a woman had ever rejected his advances before. "General Wattana has twice the army you do. Outfitted and trained soldiers, not drug runners and thugs. *He* is not afraid to accept aid from China. How do you imagine you can defeat him?"

Mai's expression turned cold. "If I recall, your founding fathers were outnumbered as well," she said. "We will prevail because we have the people's support and because our cause is right."

The American clasped his palms in a *wai* and bowed deeply. "Your Majesty."

He retreated backwards out of the room.

As soon as the door closed, Mai turned to look at Kit.

"They just want the domination drug," Kit said. "You know they do."

She held his gaze. "How *dare* you," she intoned. Her words resonated in the room, ringing with power, though she used no chemical to enhance them. "You were given no leave to speak. You open your mouth when you should be silent."

Kit felt the blood rush from his face. He saw, with a sudden sickening clarity, what he had just done. He had meant to defend her glory, to show this proud American that just because she was holding court in a hotel lobby didn't mean she wasn't a true queen. But in doing so, he hadn't treated her like a true queen.

She was the monarch of Thailand. By hundreds of years of law and sacred tradition, no one spoke in her presence unless she invited them to speak. He had not only violated those laws; he had spoken over her. He had spoken *for* her.

He threw himself to the ground. He pressed his face into the worn carpet and stretched his hands out in front of him, like any other supplicant to the crown. "Forgive me, your Majesty," he said. "I have offended. Whatever punishment you think right, I will double it."

"A science minister does not make pronouncements on foreign policy," she said. "And no man speaks for the queen."

Kit's cheeks burned. "Yes, your Majesty. I spoke out of turn. I spoke from the heart, but it is your heart which is the heart of Thailand." He pressed his face more firmly into the carpet.

"Look at me," she said.

Slowly, fearfully, he lifted his head to look at her face. She gazed down on him in regal fury. Then a tiny smile broke through her expression.

"Kittipoom Chongsuttanamanee," she declared, her clear voice ringing out again. "We hereby grant you the honorary rank of Brigadier General of the Royal Thai Army."

Kit rose slowly. "I don't deserve that. I'm not even—"

"You dare to cross my word again?"

He clamped his mouth shut.

"It's not a matter of what you *deserve*," she said. "If you're going to speak like that, then you'd better have a rank to put some authority behind it."

He bowed deeply. "Your Majesty."

"General Chongsuttanamanee," she said. "I value your advice. But if you dare to speak for me again, I will banish you from Thailand forever. Do you understand?"

"Yes, your Majesty."

"Good. Then your career as a royal officer will be a long and proud one."

Kit didn't mention that the Thai Army was loyal to General Wattana, and the Red Wa fighters who worked for Mai wouldn't care if he called himself a general. He was already starting to second-guess his rash outburst to the American emissary. After all, the man was right. If their goal was to run an organized crime ring, they had all the resources they would need. But to seize power and hold the government? They were hopelessly outgunned.

"What if the American was right?" Kit said. "What if we can't win without them?"

Mai shook her head. "He might be. But you are right, too. Winning under those terms would be no victory at all."

One of the Daughters of the Queen entered the room. "Majesty, the woman you asked about is here."

Mai's lips spread wide in a blinding smile. She turned to Arinya. "Our next guest will be of particular interest to you, I think."

Arinya looked at Kit questioningly, but he shrugged. He had no idea what mysterious guest this could be.

"I've had people out searching since the day we met," Mai said. "They finally found her."

Arinya's eyes grew wide. When Kit saw the young woman who stepped hesitantly into the room, he saw the resemblance and understood at once. Arinya shrieked and ran forward to envelop her in a fierce embrace. Kit and Mai stood by, watching, until Arinya finally released her and wiped tears from her face.

"Kit," Arinya said. "This is my sister, Chuasiri Tavaranan."

Kit gave a polite *wai* in greeting, which Chuasiri returned. "Very pleased to meet you," he said.

Arinya's sister had been taken three years earlier, caught up in the sex trafficking trade. Arinya had mourned her, not knowing if she was alive or dead and not expecting to find out. For all she knew, Chuasiri had been shipped to Europe or America. The police were no help at all. There had been nothing she could do.

"We found her in a Burmese army camp," Mai said. "She's safe now. Like the others, she'll need a lot of help to heal, but she'll be able to do so near people who love her."

Kit hadn't known Chuasiri before, but he guessed she hadn't been as thin before as she was now. She was almost gaunt, with a hunched posture and hair drawn forward to cover much of her face. Seeing Arinya, though, she smiled hesitantly, and her hand slipped into her sister's and held fast.

"I can't believe this is real," Arinya said. "Thank you. Thank you so much."

"We may not save them all," Mai said, her voice hard. "But we'll try."

Kit looked at her with admiration bordering on worship. Mai had done the impossible. Everyone accepted the sale and slavery of thousands of Thai girls a year as if it were a natural law. Sad, but unavoidable. The gang lords were above the law, the police in their pay, the government impotent. What could be done?

The moment Mai had seen the domination drug, she had known what it could do. She took it as an opportunity to make a difference, and she'd toppled an empire. She had freed thousands from slavery, founded an organization to help them reintegrate with society, and given many of them jobs working for her.

She was unstoppable. The Thai people adored her. Kit didn't care how many more troops General Wattana had. Mai would win their hearts and take her rightful place on the throne.

CHAPTER SIX

Samira couldn't get enough of watching Charlie. Even with all she knew about theropod dinosaurs, it amazed her how birdlike he was. He hopped and strutted and preened and pecked, like a big, beautiful, flightless bird. She was seeing a genuine dinosaur. It was something she'd dreamed of doing her whole life, but knew would never, ever happen. Yet now it had.

Not just a dinosaur, either, but apparently an intelligent creature, even though they had no real way to communicate. A *person*, in the broadest sense of that word. What did he think of where he was and what was happening? Did he know how much time had passed? It seemed unlikely. He just knew he was a prisoner. It wasn't right to keep a thinking person locked up like this, but they could hardly let him go free.

Beth didn't spend nearly as much time here. Her true love was statistical modeling, so she had dived into the data, contrasting Charlie's movements and anatomy with existing models. She didn't like wearing hazmat suits, and preferred computers over people anyway. Samira had always been more of a behaviorist, and she gravitated to the chair in front of his cage, just watching Charlie and writing down what he did.

Most of the time, what he did was sit very still and watch her back.

She tried using imitation to see if she could establish some kind of sign communication. If he made a clear, deliberate movement that she could imitate, she would do it back to him. When he wasn't moving, she would attempt a deliberate movement of her own to see if Charlie would parrot it back. He never did. His sharp eyes would track the motion, but he made no movement in response.

"We have to learn to communicate," Samira said.

"You're welcome to pursue that line of research," Paula said. "Just gaining a better understanding of how they communicated with each other would be valuable."

"If we can capture the scents he produces in different situations, we could use a mass spectrometer, try to break them down into component chemicals. With enough data about what the scents are composed of, maybe we could understand how the pieces combine to form the whole."

"That's a tall order," Paula said. "If you were my graduate student, I'd tell you to bite off something smaller."

Samira shrugged. "The basis of a scent language has to be straightforward, right? The word for meat is the smell of meat. The word for urine is the smell of urine. More sophisticated concepts get built up by combining simple ones, like with hieroglyphs or Chinese characters."

"Maybe. But that simple foundation may be complicated by so many layers that it's hard to tell. Even if it's not, though, how are you going to test it? With visual or audio data, we can digitize it and reproduce pictures and sounds whenever we want. We don't have the technology to reproduce smells. You might be able to break them down and identify components, but we can't easily put them together to communicate. Even if you could understand what he's saying—which is a big if— you wouldn't be able to talk back."

Eventually, they called it a day and exited through the

pressure doors. "Have you considered pumping our own personal scents into the room?" Samira asked. "That way he could smell us without being able to dominate us. If his primary sense is smell, then that could help him get to know us as individuals."

"It's a thought," Paula said. "Though some may question if we want him to know our scent. That's a predator in there, and an incredibly smart one."

"If what you're saying is true, it might be a *person* in there."

Paula unzipped Samira's hazmat suit and helped her climb out of it. "I know. I even think of Wallace and Marcy as people." Wallace was Samira's red-and-green macaw, and Marcy was a crow Paula kept and studied at the avian lab at the University of Colorado. "I feel bad keeping him caged. But it's not like we can let him loose to forage in the Rocky Mountains. The best we can do for him is feed and care for him and learn to communicate as best as we can."

It felt good to get out of the claustrophobic suit. Samira wiped sweat from her face and scratched her scalp. Funny how many itches you noticed when there was no opportunity to scratch them.

A man came in through the other door. He was several inches shorter than Samira, but so muscled he had to hold his arms slightly out from his body instead of letting them hang straight. A tattoo of a Chinese dragon started with its rear legs and tail on his left forearm, wound its sinuous way up to his bicep and disappeared under a tight T-shirt sleeve, only to reappear on the right bicep and end with a fire-breathing head. She wondered if the effect continued across his back. His T-shirt said LIFT in large block letters over a pair of barbells.

"Samira, this is Alex," Paula said. "Alex, Samira is the newest addition to our team."

He held out a hand. "Welcome. Paula's told me all about you."

Samira fought the instinct to press her hands together in a *wai* and shook his outstretched hand instead. He looked freshly showered—probably just came from the gym—and she felt suddenly conscious of her sweat-slicked hair and skin. Samira was wary of people who exercised so much they wore T-shirts to tell you about it. In her experience, such people spent most of any conversation talking about their favorite new workouts or nutritional epiphanies, as if pointing out how much they were winning at the game of life and you were losing. It was probably unfair of her to stereotype him like that, but she couldn't help her first impression.

"So you're the guy Charlie nearly ate for breakfast," she said.

Alex grinned. "Yeah, well, apparently I wasn't so appetizing once he got a whiff of me."

He climbed into his hazmat suit and Paula and Samira made their way out.

"I just wish there was a way I could understand Charlie," Samira said.

"Come with me." Paula pushed gray hair back from her eyes, which sparkled with mischievous delight. "I'll show you our memory collection."

"YOU'RE NOT GOING to tell me what I'm going to see?" Samira asked.

The technician handed her a clear plastic anesthetic face mask with a tube dangling from it. "Just strap that on and lie back," Paula said. "There's really no way to explain. It's like what you saw in Thailand, but a different memory. You have to experience it for yourself."

"Why does that not make me feel better?"

"Just relax."

A medical bed stood in the room next to a large white

machine that looked like a piece of hospital equipment. Samira sat down reluctantly on the bed.

"Just lie back," Paula said, as cheerful as ever.

"You're scaring me," Samira said. "If it weren't you, I wouldn't be agreeing to this."

"You'll be a bit more scared before this is done."

"Oh great, thanks."

The technician slid a Velcro strap around her wrist, pinning her arm to the bed rail. Samira yanked at it. "What is that for?"

"It's for your own safety," Paula said. "You remember from Thailand, right? It's terrifying at first. But it's safe. I've done it countless times. Andy here has done it. Lots of people have."

The technician wrapped her other wrist. "Paula? Let me out of here. I'm not doing this until you tell me what I'm going to see."

Paula put a soft hand on her head. "Samira. It's better this way. Trust me."

She looked into Paula's motherly blue eyes, crinkled at the edges from a lifetime of smiles. "Okay," she said. She swallowed hard. "Get it over with."

Paula signaled to the technician, who turned a dial. A hiss came from the machine, and into the face mask poured a sudden, sharp smell...and a moment of stark terror as a maniraptor loomed suddenly over the bed at her. She panicked, screaming into the mask and trying to pull away, but the straps held her fast. Then the room disappeared.

SHE WAS THROWN INTO CHAOS. *She stood in a canyon shaded by a giant sequoia tree. The canyon was full of maniraptors.* She *was a maniraptor.*

A riot of smells swept through the space, many of them forceful and angry. The leaders of the roosts were expressing their displeasure. Most of them, she thought, were idiots.

A scrawny male from Ocean Roost had just told them all that an asteroid was coming to destroy the world. They thought because he was small and male and brought unwelcome news that it couldn't possibly be true. It was a political maneuver by Ocean Roost, they thought. A ploy to distract them from more pressing matters, or to give Ocean more centrality and prestige.

The female leader from Ocean Roost stood on the high perch, trying to communicate to the crowd, but no one was paying attention. The problem was that they really did believe what the scrawny male had said, but they refused to admit it. They were scared, all of them, and the stink of terror pervaded all of the angry denials.

The male had spoken of modifying their species to survive the coming apocalypse. For most of the females, that was tantamount to sacrilege, suggesting that they were little more than animals. Modification was something you did to fashion a tool. Females did not modify themselves.

Idiots. They would rather die than give up their pride.

The crowd of dignitaries started to move. Anyone who stayed in one place in an argument like this would influence only those closest to them. To sway a crowd, you had to move through it, discharging your scent as widely as possible to make your opinion known. Until now, representatives had stayed in their own roost groups, but now the crowd surged, snarling and snapping and spreading their views. Physical fighting was unlikely, but the air could get pretty charged with violent pheromones.

These were high ranking leaders with scent markers that commanded fear and obedience. She was a minor functionary, small for a female, but she hadn't gotten as far as she had by deferring to authority. She leaped into the fray, pushing through bodies and spraying her opinion in every direction.

The danger is real, *she argued.* We must do whatever it takes to survive.

Sometimes she could influence higher-ranked females through her intelligence and logic, but everyone around her was frightened. Deep genetic instincts made them run to the more powerful and dominant without considering if they were right or not. The swirling arguments moved gradually toward consensus, with her dissents increasingly overwhelmed.

She caught the scent of another dissenter, mild but distinct, and moved through the crowd in that direction. She found a male from her own roost, a brilliant researcher and one of the best modifiers she knew. "Come with me," she told him.

They circled around the edge of the canyon toward where the representatives of the Ocean Roost had originally congregated. They found the scrawny male who had told the gathered council about the impending catastrophe.

She threw out a command scent to get his attention, and he leaped in the air as if she'd prodded him with a claw.

"I am called Distant Rain Sweeping Towards Home as Night Falls," she told him.

The male touched his head to the ground. "May your teeth be sharp and your claws strong."

"This is Fear Stink of Injured Mammal Limping Through the Sand," she said.

"We think you're right," said Fear Stink. "Altering our bodies is the only way to survive this long-term."

The scrawny male gave off a whiff of astonishment. "You believe me?"

Rain conveyed her assent. "What kind of modifications do you think we need?"

THE CANYON DISAPPEARED. Disoriented, Samira thrashed, snapping her jaws in every direction. Slowly, she took in the fluorescent lights, the drop ceiling, the machine and the technician and Paula, standing just where they had been. It seemed like hours had passed.

"What," she said. "How long…?"

"Only a moment," Paula said. "It just feels like longer."

The technician released her arms. Samira sat up, still a bit dizzy. "It seemed so real."

"It was real. It just happened to a maniraptor who died sixty-six million years ago."

Samira shook her head in astonishment. "It was amazing. The way they used scent to reach consensus, like hundreds of people all talking at once and somehow understanding what everyone was saying."

"It's a radically different communication mechanism," Paula agreed.

"I would have thought it was a bad one, compared to sound," Samira said. "Smell lingers in the air. It's like trying to have a conversation when everything you say echoes over and over again—you couldn't keep it all straight. But they seemed to have turned that attribute into an advantage."

"Brains are incredibly good at doing exactly that," Paula said. "You haven't learned to handle the echoing scenario, because that doesn't happen in normal life. But you can understand the person across from you in a crowded restaurant, even though there are ten other tables of people talking, music playing, clinking silverware, and the hum of air conditioning. Your brain has no trouble filtering out the important from the unimportant."

Samira stood up, then grabbed the bed to steady herself.

"Take your time," Paula said. "Our brains aren't used to experiences like this."

Samira took deep breaths, trying to think through the things she'd seen. "Their mode of communication defined the kind of technology they developed," she said. "Instead of a printing press or the telephone, they expanded the long-lasting nature of scent communication from marking their territory to sharing memories directly with others and storing them chemically for future generations."

Paula's expression grew wistful. "They must have had vast stores of those memories. We only have the tiniest sampling."

"How many of these do you have?"

"Close to three hundred."

Samira whistled. "Nothing like what they used to have, I'm sure, but that's still a lot."

"The problem is, it's a limited supply. Every time someone breathes in one of these memories, we have a little less of the very complicated neurochemical cocktail that produces it. So I'll have to ask you to take some time now and write down, in as complete detail as possible, everything that you saw. We have to translate it into our own form of long-term storage, or we'll lose it."

"You said you take scent chemical from Charlie twice a day. Don't you get more memories when you do that?"

Paula shook her head. "That's just the base chemical. It will produce the same sense of fear and will work to dominate others, but it doesn't encode any memories. Presumably he could share memories with us if he wanted to, but he hasn't."

"Of course not. We've got him trapped behind glass and we're wearing hazmat suits. He couldn't share memories with us if he wanted to."

"And for the time being, we'll keep it that way."

Samira let go of the bed and took a tentative step. The dizziness was gone. "But how does it work at all?" she asked. "How does a chemical meant for maniraptor brains get interpreted by ours? I wouldn't have expected our brains to have the biological hardware to turn scent data into experience."

Paula smiled. "Have I told you how nice it is to finally have you working with us? You ask good questions. Are you familiar with Noam Chomsky's theory of Universal Grammar?"

"Um, maybe? The idea that the structure of language has a genetic basis?"

"Essentially, yes. He posited—and a lot of the linguistic community agrees with him—that the foundations of language are innate in human genetics. If so, then maybe these memories communicate at that foundational level."

"But we're not descended from dinosaurs. We're on a radically different evolutionary branch."

Paula shrugged. "Maybe our speech has more in common with animal communication than we think. Maybe Chomsky's theory is true because it's the underlying structure of memory formation and storage that's common to all creatures with a cerebral cortex."

"In the memory I saw in Thailand, the males had another mode of speech," she said. "A spoken one."

Paula's eyebrows shot up. "You never mentioned that before."

"I didn't know about any of this then," she said with some heat. "I didn't know you were involved. I was debriefed by a soldier and told to forget I was ever there."

"Sorry about that," Paula said. "I did what I could. It wasn't easy to convince them to read you in." She leaned forward. "Tell me about this spoken language, though. They communicated with sound? Not just emotional expression, but a true language?"

"It was just the males," Samira said. "It was considered a bit crude, not something the more cultured females would use. They looked down on it as a less capable and sophisticated form of communication than scent."

"Intriguing."

"You never encountered that in any of these other memories?"

"No. The vast majority of the memories are from a female perspective. It's never come up. There are other species that vocalize in various ways, as animals, but our maniraptor friends are generally silent."

SAMIRA BEGAN TALKING TO CHARLIE. The room was split roughly in half, with the lab on one side and Charlie's enclosure on the other. The lab included the air handling system to manage Charlie's air supply or pump in the gas that sedated him, as well as the mechanism to open the enclosure to give him food or access him for any reason. As such, it shared Charlie's environment, and so anyone in the lab had to wear hazmat gear. In addition, an elevated observation room above the lab allowed visibility into what was going on below without breathing the same air. It meant Samira didn't have to wear a hazmat suit to see Charlie, or even to talk to him, but she always did anyway. She wanted to be in the same room with him, on his level. Even though her voice had to be transmitted through a microphone in either case, she wanted to be close enough to him that he could see her lips move and get a better sense of connection.

She said the same things every day. She repeated her name and his name. She identified her body parts. She held up objects and told him what they were called. While she did so, sensitive chemical sensors in his enclosure characterized the chemical composition of the air. She had hoped he would understand and respond with a lexicon of his own, allowing them to build up a shared language, even if it used different senses. But he never responded. He just watched her impassively, giving no indication that he comprehended her purpose at all.

Even so, she began to see his personality, to glimpse the individual inside the creature. He paid much more attention to her, for instance, than to any of the other researchers in the lab. Paula he gave some notice to, tracking her progress if she moved around the room. Alex he paid no attention to at all. He clearly resented being put to sleep. When they pumped gas into the enclosure, he crouched as far away from it as possible, growling through bared teeth.

She realized she still thought of him like she did about

Wallace, however, or any of the clever birds in Paula's ornithology center. Not as a person, not really. It surprised her how reluctant her mind was to accept him as a thinking being. She had seen through his eyes, after all. She'd experienced his memories. Despite that, looking at this prehistoric bird-reptile, part of her still wanted to draw a sharp line between humanity and him and say: *We are what matters. You are just an animal.*

Was it really just humans' inability to understand other modes of communication that prevented them from recognizing intelligence in other species? Despite all she knew, she found it hard to accept Charlie. Were there only two examples, now, of reasoning, self-aware species? Or was that a false category? Were elephants and dolphins and ravens and parrots and dogs and cats aware of themselves as individuals? Were chickens? Mosquitos? Microbes? It seemed like an important moral distinction to make, but she wasn't sure how to draw the line. She had been raised to think that only humans had souls, but she had always assumed that others were possible. Aliens from another planet, for instance.

Face to face with an example, though, she wanted to deny it. If that was a person on the other side of the glass, she had responsibilities to him beyond simple scientific exploration. Paula was right that he couldn't just be released, but it meant they couldn't just treat him like a lab animal either. It meant that what he wanted mattered.

CHAPTER SEVEN

S amira started to lose track of the world outside the facility. She worked late nights, worked weekends, often slept at the lab. She and Beth drove in together, but sometimes it didn't seem worth the commute back to their apartment, and she told Beth to go ahead without her.

After several weeks of this, Beth showed up in the observation room at five o'clock and insisted that Samira come with her.

"It's early yet," Samira said. "He'll be fed tonight. I'm always here when he's fed."

"He ate food before you even knew he existed," Beth said. "*You* need food, too. You're not eating well. I made *misir wat* last night; we just have to warm it up and eat it."

It was Samira's favorite Ethiopian comfort food, and Beth knew it. "You could have brought it to the lab and warmed it up here," Samira said.

"No, I specifically did not do that. The whole point of making it was to lure you home for an evening. I'm worried about you. You're working twenty hours a day sometimes. It's not healthy. Wallace misses you, too."

That got her. Wallace, her pet macaw, was a social creature who needed personal attention to thrive. She'd been neglecting him to spend time with Charlie. She'd even considered asking if she could keep him in the facility, but where exactly that would work wasn't clear. Space was at a premium underground, and a macaw was too loud and demanding to keep in someone's workspace.

Samira's first instinct was to get angry. She was an adult; she didn't need Beth to mother-hen her. Any paleontologist would sell their right arm for an opportunity like this. Of course she was going to give it everything she had. She didn't need her sister to scold her about pet care.

She recognized that instinct, though, and took a deep breath before she lashed out. Beth loved this work, too, and she loved Samira. She might be overprotective, but that was no reason to attack her. "Okay," she said. "I'll come. But I'm staying late tomorrow."

Beth beamed. "Good choice. I didn't want to have to overpower you."

"Just a minute," Samira said. She faced the cage. As usual, Charlie watched her intently. "Goodbye," she said. "I have to leave. I'll see you tomorrow."

Charlie made no reaction.

"That's it, then," Samira said. "Let's go."

"I'M NOT A WORKAHOLIC," Samira said, as they climbed the flight of stairs and Beth unlocked the door to their apartment. "I'm dedicated. There's a difference."

"Do you even know what day it is?" Beth asked.

"Of course, I do. It's, um…" She wasn't actually sure.

The door swung open. Samira had just a moment to register that the lights were on and there were people in their apartment when her parents threw their arms in the air and shouted, "Surprise!"

Samira stood there, stunned, as her mom leaned in and kissed her cheek. "Happy birthday, honey."

Beth smirked. "What day did you say it was?"

"Okay, maybe I haven't been paying attention," Samira said.

Her dad put an arm around her and led her into the room. Streamers hung from the ceiling, and a two-tier chocolate birthday cake sat on the counter with her name written inexpertly with icing.

When she and Beth were growing up in Ethiopia, birthday celebrations among their friends were rare. Birthdays would be remembered with a little popcorn or Dabo bread, if they were remembered at all. As they got older, though, at least in Addis Ababa, the tradition had spread, in imitation of the Western celebration they saw in Hollywood movies. So despite their cross-cultural background, their birthday memories were distinctly American: cakes, candles, streamers, presents, and the Happy Birthday song, which Beth and her parents now sang with gusto in Amharic. As the last *melkam lidet* echoed around the room, Wallace squawked his agreement, and Samira laughed and hugged each of them.

"Thank you," she said. "This is wonderful."

While shoveling delicious spoonfuls of spicy red lentils into her mouth, Samira had to admit Beth was right. She was overwhelmed and overtired, and a night of good food and good company was exactly what she needed. She didn't even mind that the company was her parents, despite their fraught relationship. It meant she couldn't talk about work, and that was a good thing. She realized that despite the incredible privilege she felt at getting to work with Charlie, she also felt an incredible pressure not to screw it up.

"How have you guys been?" she asked her parents.

"Overwhelmed," her dad said. "This is a nice break."

"We've been plugged into the virus relief efforts," her mom explained. "Packaging up medical supplies and nonperishables, figuring out what kind of supply routes we can use to reliably get it into the hands of the people who need it."

Samira realized she hadn't read the news in weeks. Her parents were talking about the Julian virus that Gabby's mother had died from in Argentina. "Is it getting bad?" she asked. "I haven't really been paying attention."

"Spread to West Africa now," her dad said. "Cases in Nigeria, Niger, Benin. Lagos has it the worst. It spreads as aggressively as COVID, but kills more people than Ebola. And it spreads through animals, at least most mammals and birds. They don't know how to stop it."

It was just like her parents, to dive in headfirst to any humanitarian need around the globe. Sometimes it felt like they cared about children across the world more than they cared about her, but she pushed that thought aside. It was her birthday. They were here. They loved her, and they were showing that love right now. She could work through her insecurities another day.

She took her dad's hand. "Just don't go rushing off into a plague zone to help, will you?"

He laughed awkwardly and traded a look with her mom. "We're staying right here," he said. Though clearly they had thought about it.

"Good," Beth said. "I don't think ophthalmology is what those people need right now."

Her dad laughed. "Right," he said. "We can probably help more from here. We have contacts, we can organize relief efforts, work the system. Not everyone knows how to do that."

"You sound like you're trying to convince yourself," Samira said.

"You know your dad," Mom said. "Thinks he's still thirty-five. Wherever the need is greatest, that's where he wants to be."

Samira did know. It was part of what made her relationship with her parents so difficult for her. They were heroes.

They were willing to sacrifice anything for other people and had spent their career literally saving lives. Samira herself had been one of those saved lives, adopted off the streets when she had no one and nothing. She struggled not to feel like she was just one more of her parents' third-world conquests.

She shook her head. *Not now.*

"I think he is still thirty-five," she said. "I think he could still run a marathon."

Her father huffed out a laugh, but he really did look remarkably hale for his sixty years. He stooped a little more than he used to, and his beard had gone gray, but his skin was unlined and he had more energy than many half his age.

Her mom put her hands to her cheeks, which were much more noticeably lined with age. "Unlike me," she said. "I never should have married a younger man."

Her mom was only eight months older than her dad, but it had been a running joke since Beth and Samira were little. The conversation continued that way, retreading old and comfortable paths, talking about nothing and yet communicating everything. Samira felt more relaxed around them than she had in years.

When it came time for presents and one of the packages felt like a book, Samira cringed, expecting a Creationist screed or some kind of Christian book she would feel guilt-tripped into reading. It wouldn't have been the first time. Instead, it was *The Great Dying: A New Look at the Permian Extinction*, by Elena Benitez, Gabby's mother. Elena had written it before her death, but it had only recently been published. If Samira had visited a bookstore with cash in her pocket, it's probably the book she would have come home with.

"Wow, thanks!" she said, flipping it to the back to see a small picture of Elena along with blurbs and a description. "This is great."

"Beth suggested it," her mom said. "I hope you enjoy it."

AFTER THEY LEFT, and she and Beth were alone in the apartment, Samira's thoughts veered back to work, and she couldn't stop herself from talking about it. Two hours was as much of a break as her mind would let her have.

"He responds now, when he sees me," she said. "He gets more alert, comes to the front of the enclosure. I think I'm making a connection."

"No actual communication, though?" Beth asked.

"I have to gain his trust. That takes time."

"Maybe he is responding. If he was sending scents at you, how would you even know?"

"Well, we've got chemical sensors sampling the air in his enclosure. If there was something different to smell, we'd detect it. We might not know what it meant, but we would at least know something had changed."

"But he knows you can't smell him, right? Because of your suits. So he would know he couldn't reach you."

"That's true, I guess. I'm not sure how to change that, though, short of giving myself over to be eaten."

"You should stop by the anatomy lab," Beth said. "We've got a complete digital model of his musculature now. We know exactly how much force he can create with his jaw, how high he can jump, everything."

"That's great," Samira said.

Beth frowned. "Don't minimize my work, Sami."

"I wasn't."

"You were. I can tell when you mean it."

Samira slumped. "I'm sorry. It is important, I really do think that. Capturing anatomical data from a real dinosaur? It's phenomenal."

"But?"

"But it makes me mad. You're collecting all this data, but for what? They won't let you publish. It just goes into a black hole. Some classified data store that will never see the light of day."

Beth gave a little smile. "Well," she said. "You're the confrontational one. Maybe you should do something about that."

"Yeah," Samira said. "Maybe I should."

FIRST THING THE NEXT MORNING, she took up the issue with the commander of the facility, a civilian CIA agent named Adam Hunt. Hunt told her it was classified, and that there was nothing to talk about.

"But I don't understand why it's secret at all," Samira said. "Science doesn't work well behind closed doors. There's a process of peer reviews and repeated experiments leading to scientific consensus. Those few of us here can't think of every-thing and we can't know everything."

"It's a matter of national security," Hunt said, steepling his fingers. "I think you know that. There's a capacity for mind control here, and we don't want that falling into the wrong hands. Do you want the enemies of America having that power?"

"But the Chinese already have it, right? And if they know we already have it, then we'll know not to attack each other. Isn't it *better* for them to know what we can do? The more they know our capabilities, the less inclined they'll be to try and start a fight."

Hunt gave her an unreadable stare before finally replying. "I apologize, Dr. Shannon. I forget that you are not a profes-sional, and these concepts are new to you. If they know what our capabilities are, then they will know if theirs are better, and where we are vulnerable. They will be able to devise ways of neutralizing our advantages. Consider which would be easier: to play chess against an opponent the standard way, or to play against an opponent whose pieces are invisible? You may suspect that your strength is equal to his, but you won't know where his strongest pieces are located or how to counter his moves effectively. That is the art of counter-intelligence. To render both our strengths and weaknesses as invisible to our adversaries as possible."

"IT'S ABOUT TIME," Alex said. "Where have you been?"

"I had a meeting with Hunt. Why? Did you need me?"

Samira had just suited up and entered the lab. Alex sat above in the observation room, working on one of the computers. He stood at the window and pressed the button on a microphone to speak to her.

"Not me. Your biggest fan." Alex's T-shirt of the day featured a parody of the familiar "Road to Homo Sapiens" illustration, showing the progression from a chimpanzee to a man through various intermediate stages, except that the final stage was a bodybuilder holding a barbell aloft. Despite his shirts and musculature, he never talked about his gym work-outs—or really anything about his personal life—and probably spent as many hours on the job as Samira did.

"My biggest fan?"

"Charlie. He's been saying your name."

"*What?*"

"He's been standing at the window, right where you usually talk to him, since early this morning, repeating what sounds an awful lot like your name."

She looked and sure enough, there he was, looking agitated and rubbing his head against the protofeather fluff on his side. A dusting of fluff drifted near his feet.

"You're kidding about the name part, though, right?"

"No," Alex said, and then Charlie squawked, loud and shrill.

MEE-KAA!

"See?"

Samira eyed Alex in the observation deck, suspicious. "That doesn't sound very much like—"

MEE-KAA! HA-MEE-KAA!

A thrill shot through her, despite her skepticism. It wasn't that close, but if you tilted your head just right and *believed...*

"How do you know that's my name?" Samira asked. "He could be saying anything, or nothing at all."

"He started at eight, right when you usually get in. He keeps coming to the edge of his cage, looking at the chair where you usually sit to talk to him, and screeching your name."

Samira stared at Charlie, amazed. Her own name was one of the most frequent words she repeated to him, pointing to herself as she said it. Had he actually understood its meaning and learned how to reproduce it?

HA-MEE-KAA!

"I think he's in love." Alex said. "You could do worse, I guess."

"I have done worse."

She approached the cage and took her usual seat. She placed her hand on her chest as she always did and said, "Samira." Then she pointed to him and said, "Charlie."

HA-MEE-KAA! Charlie said.

"Okay," she said. "It's a start."

She studied his appearance through the double barrier of facemask and glass. Had his rich brown coloring lost some of its luster since she'd first seen him? There were a few bare patches where he'd gnawed his own feathers away. Parrots in captivity would pluck themselves if they didn't get enough fresh air or sunlight or had other sources of stress or anxiety. His cage was hardly an ideal habitat, and he was isolated from others of his kind.

The more intelligent he was, the worse his predicament

seemed. Did he understand that he was the only living member of his species? Did he know how much time had passed? It seemed unlikely that he could. But then, what did he think humans were? How would she react if she woke up in prison, alone, surrounded by aliens who stared at her all day and spoke gibberish? *Terrified* wouldn't even begin to describe it.

They had to show him they were his friends, not his captors. That they were there to help him.

"Alex, I want to go into the cage with him."

Alex made a choking sound. "No, I don't think you do."

"Don't tell me what I want. *You* went in with him."

"I went in when I thought it was asleep, and it nearly killed me. You saw what it does to the animals we give it for food. Don't let it get your guard down by mimicking your sounds or anticipating your arrival. That could just be instinct, evolved as a hunting strategy to lure prey or predict where to find it."

Samira was tired of men deciding what was best for her. "Some people are more than just evolutionary programming," she said. "Should I assume that because of yours, all you want to do is get me into bed?"

Alex flushed red and raised his hands in protest. "Geez, Samira, no."

"Then don't assume the only thing Charlie wants to do is eat me."

He gritted his teeth and made a placating gesture. "It's your life. But it's me who has to drag out your body and clean up the blood if you're wrong, and I don't want to do that. Besides, it's not up to either of us. You need to get Paula's okay."

"And you're going to call her if I go in, aren't you?"

"No, I'm going to press the emergency call button, and soldiers are going to rush in here, followed closely by Adam Hunt, and you'll probably never see Charlie again. Not to mention that there's at least a fifty percent chance that if he kills a human someone will make the decision to put him down, last of his species or not. Don't push me on this. I don't want any dead bodies on my watch."

She clenched her fists. He was probably right. But they had to find a way to put Charlie at ease. He was sickening, and would probably get worse if they couldn't relieve some of the stress. The only way she could see to do that was to develop a relationship with him, and what kind of relationship could they have with a thick sheet of glass and a Hazmat suit between them? He couldn't smell her, he could barely see her, and all he could hear was what was piped through a loud-speaker system. It was amazing he had learned to associate the sound of her voice as coming from her at all.

"Alex?"

"Yes?" He sounded wary.

"How hard would it be to pipe some of those smells we collected into his cage?"

"You mean the memory odors?"

"Yeah. I don't mean *his* memories, though—memories from other maniraptors. So maybe he wouldn't feel quite so alone."

Alex cocked an eyebrow. "Technology-wise, it's no problem. I could do it. I think you'd better run it past Paula, though."

She huffed her frustration. "You're not going to let me get away with anything, are you?"

"Nope." His smile popped out again. "As soon as you realize I'm the king around here, we'll get along much better."

"Sounds to me like Paula's the one in charge."

"Prince, then. Or prime minister."

"How about loyal bulldog?"

"Okay," he said. "I'll take it."

CHAPTER EIGHT

P akasit Paknikorn sat hunched on his bunk and tried to disappear. He had thought about taking his own life many times since the day he emptied his shotgun into his brother-in-law's chest, but he didn't have the courage to actually go through with it. He took out his photo of Kwanjai, worn soft and cracked. She would be eight years old now. A whole year since he'd disappeared from her life. He wondered if she even thought of him anymore.

The men in the barracks around him shouted and whooped at a porn film playing on an old television bolted to the wall. Aroon, who could never shut up at the best of times, narrated every move on screen at the top of his lungs. Pak couldn't look. He couldn't see the girls without thinking of Kwanjai.

"What about you, Pak?" Aroon shouted. "Which one of them would you do, if you could?"

Pak turned away. His bunk creaked dangerously as Aroon dropped his bulk onto it. "Come on, what do you think? Blonde or brunette?" Pak could smell the stink of *lao khao* on his breath.

"I have a daughter," Pak said.

"So? I have a wife, but I'm still alive, aren't I?"

"Bet your wife can't do *that!*" yelled another man, looking at the screen.

"That your daughter?" Aroon asked, snatching the photo from Pak's hand.

"Give it back," Pak said.

"Oooh, bet she'll be hot in a few years," Aroon said.

Pak punched him. He'd never been much of a brawler, but twenty years of farming had made his muscles hard. He connected with Aroon's jaw, sending him sprawling off the bunk and onto the floor. The room went suddenly quiet except for the obscene noises coming from the television.

Then, from the floor, Aroon started laughing. The rest of the men laughed with him, and one of them clapped Pak on the back. Pak picked up his photo from the floor and walked out.

THE NIGHT AIR WAS COLD, but he didn't care. Life in the barracks was growing worse. When Princess Sirindhorn had walked into camp like an avenging goddess and took command, he'd hoped that might be the beginning of something good.

For a while, it had been. She'd freed the camp's women and stopped the smuggling. She'd turned the Red Wa army into her own fighting force, and set many of the men to honest physical labor, rebuilding towns they'd destroyed, working the nearby farms, and distributing food around the countryside.

The men had adored her at first. They took to their new lives willingly, giving up violence and drugs and abuse to work hard, even taking orders from women they had once enslaved. Pak wasn't an educated man, but he was smart enough to realize it had something to do with fossils like the one he'd found and the chemical labs that processed them.

But things were changing now. The men were growing restless, more vulgar and violent, more likely to ignore their work. They bragged about the women they'd assaulted, and whether their stories were true or not, it meant that whatever control the princess had claimed over them was slipping. And these were the *best* of the men who had once run the Tachileik branch of the Red Wa. The worst had died the day the princess had taken command.

"You're not like the rest of them, are you?" a voice asked.

Startled, Pak turned to see a woman leaning against the barracks wall, smoking a cigarette. He guessed she was about thirty, though she had the hardened look of many of the women that made it hard to tell.

"I hate it here," Pak admitted.

"Where's home?"

"Isan."

"Long way. How'd you end up here?"

A vision of Nikorn's dead face swam up in his memory. "I did something wrong," he said. "Unforgivable."

"Sometimes people can forgive more than you think."

He shook his head. "Not this."

They were quiet for a moment. The woman breathed out a puff of smoke that drifted away in the cold air.

The woman nodded at the photo of Kwanjai he still clutched in his hand. "Who's that? Your little girl?"

He angled the picture to show her.

"She's lovely."

"Smart, too," Pak said. "I want her to go to school. I send money home for her, but…"

"But?"

"But I don't think that's what my wife will use the money for."

It was the first time since he'd come to Tachileik that anyone had taken an interest in him. The first time he'd had an actual conversation. "How about you?" he asked.

"Oh," she said. "You know."

He thought he did. How could a woman who'd been through what she probably had talk about forgiveness? Some things could never be forgiven. Though he'd started to think even enduring the hatred of his family and village might be better than staying here. He could at least be part of Kwanjai's life again.

The woman breathed out another puff of smoke. "Maybe if you won the lottery, they'd accept you back."

Pak chuckled. The government-run lottery was very popular in Thailand, and almost everyone played. It was commonly believed that personal tragedy increased your good luck to pick a winning number, so by that reasoning, maybe he should buy some tickets. Though he wasn't sure if the good luck worked if the calamity was of your own making.

"Money solves all problems, is that it?" he said.

The woman shrugged. "It certainly helps. I know someone with a lot of money."

"Must be nice."

"He's willing to spread some of it around. To the right people."

Pak hesitated, eyeing the woman. Their casual conversation had just taken a turn. "What would these 'right people' have to do?" he asked warily.

"Not much. Just tell him what you see. Maybe look the other way sometimes."

Pak puffed out a breath of cold air, mirroring the woman's cigarette smoke. There was no way this offer was a good one. But he felt no loyalty to the men in the barracks behind him. And what could it hurt? He could hardly sink any lower. And maybe the woman was right. Maybe with enough money, he could go home and be forgiven.

"I could use some money," he said.

She nodded. "I'll talk to him. See what we can do."

"I'll tell you one thing for free," he said. "The princess isn't going to last much longer."

"No?"

"Whatever hold she has over the men, it's slipping."

"That is very interesting," the woman said. She tossed the butt of her cigarette to the dirt and ground it out with her foot. "Do you know why?"

"There's some kind of chemical," he said. "I think she's running out. She's controlling the people at the top now, and using them to control the rest of us, but that won't work forever. These men are criminals, not soldiers. They want drugs and money and women, and if they can't get that here, they won't stay."

"Do you know where she keeps that chemical?"

He thought about the drug labs. "I think so. Some of it, anyway."

She waited expectantly.

He scuffed one shoe in the dirt. "You said something about money?"

CHAPTER NINE

"**B**ut he's suffering," Samira said. "He might even be dying. You know what it means when a bird starts plucking out its feathers. You think it's different for Charlie?"

Paula set a cup of tea on the table in front of Samira and laid her white, wrinkled hand onto Samira's smooth, dark one. "It's not a surprise. He's trapped in a tiny space, bored, scared, cut off from anything he's ever known. It's a pretty stressful situation for him."

"Then why don't you let me try to change that?"

Paula sighed. "It's a risk. I don't know what will happen if we send him those memories. I have no idea what he understands. Will he think another one of his kind is nearby, communicating with him? Will he go crazy and try to break out of his enclosure? It could ultimately be worse for him."

"Doing nothing is a risk, too. If he gets sick, we won't be able to treat him. He'll just die."

Paula took a sip of her tea. Samira let her think. Paula knew as well as she did how easily animals brought back from extinction died. Even bringing back a relatively recent animal like a Tasmanian wolf, the last of which had died in 1936, meant providing an appropriate environment for an animal whose natural habitat no longer existed. The team that had finally succeeded in raising Charlotte to adulthood had lost six Tasmanian wolves before she had finally thrived.

Tasmanian wolves were simple, though, compared to Charlie. They were mostly solitary creatures that had fed on animals that still existed in the world today. Charlie had fed on two-ton hadrosaurs. Even the chemical makeup of the atmosphere had been different in the Cretaceous, with more oxygen and less nitrogen. The most important piece, though, in Samira's opinion, was the social component. Charlie was an intelligent and highly social creature cut off from his kind. They had to address that aspect of his health, or he wasn't going to survive.

Samira was about to open her mouth to make some of those arguments when Paula nodded as if she'd been listening to her thoughts all along. "I think you're right," she said. "I've been too cautious, too afraid to make a mistake with the only specimen we will ever have. We need to communicate with him, and those scents are our best shot."

IT TOOK a lot more work than Samira anticipated to bring the scents to Charlie. The liquid that stored the memories was volatile, evaporating quickly when exposed to the air. The machine they used to aerosolize tiny amounts of it wasn't designed to be portable, and it connected to a mask made for humans. They needed to be able to pump the scent into his cage using as little as possible of the irreplaceable liquid.

After a frustrating several hours spent sterilizing all the equipment to be sure they weren't bringing in contaminants that could harm Charlie, they finally brought what they needed inside and set it up. Charlie watched warily as they hooked the tube up to his air supply.

They had chosen a memory they thought would be less traumatic than others, a scene with five maniraptors sharing meat together on a rocky beach. The male whose memory it was felt emotions of camaraderie and the hope of being respected by the group. There was some social stress involved, but nothing like the panic and trauma of the asteroid strike. Of course, the scene might have more significance to Charlie than they realized, but they couldn't control that.

"Hello, Charlie," she said, as she always did. "This is Samira."

HA-MEE-KAA!

"That's right. We brought you something. I hope you like it."

Paula fiddled with the controls, the hazmat suit making her movements clumsy, then flipped a switch. "Okay," she said. "Here goes nothing."

At first, Charlie made no response. Then his eyes widened and his nostrils flared. He tilted his head up, his muscles taut as if to attack.

"It's a male scent marker," Paula said. "It shouldn't be a threat to him. At least if we understand it right."

Without warning, Charlie lunged, his body careening through the air, claws and teeth first, like the fearsome predator he was. He crashed into the grate that the scent was coming from, tearing at the metal, gouging it with his claws and trying to get purchase with his teeth. He screeched a sound they'd never heard him make before, full of emotion. Samira knew he was an alien creature with wildly different means of communication, but it wasn't hard to hear rage and longing in that sound.

"Whoa," Alex said. He sat in the observation room, watching the sensors. "Chemical readings are off the charts. He's pumping some serious alkylpyrazines into the air."

"I'm shutting it down," Paula said, reaching for the switch.

"No," Samira said. "Give him a chance. Switch to the next memory. Let him figure it out."

"He's going to hurt himself," Paula said, but she did as Samira asked.

As the next cascade of scents drifted into his cage, Charlie froze, pausing his furious clawing at the grate. His body relaxed, then slumped to the floor. He rested his head between his feet. Samira cautioned herself against anthropomorphism, but she couldn't help thinking that if he'd been human, he would be crying.

WHEN HE CAUGHT the scent marker of another maniraptor, Prey thought at first that his roost mates had come for him. He called back, flooding the air with information about his location and his captors. It didn't take long for him to realize the truth: the scents were stale, mere recorded memories. Not only that, they were quite old, judging by the quality.

The memory changed, and he saw the tangled cliff dwellings of Ocean Roost, felt the cool air, smelled salt on the breeze. Home. But he was not home. He was here, trapped by hairless mammals in a cage with invisible walls. The mammals were watching him. They were doing this. They had robbed Ocean Roost's library, and now they fed him these scents of his past life to torture him and keep him weak.

No. That wasn't right, was it? These creatures didn't know how to speak with scent. They wore costumes to prevent scent from passing from one to the other and communicated vocally, like males. They probably didn't understand what these scents meant any more than prey animals in the field understood anger or affection. But if so, why were they doing it?

The only reason he could think of was for communication. His pitiful attempts to repeat their vocalizations had failed, so they were making equally pitiful attempts to speak his language in return.

Samira was behind this, he knew it. She was different from the others. Prey had been told the names of the other creatures, but he didn't remember. The sounds were hard to hold onto; if he didn't hear it repeated many times, he often forgot it later. But he didn't care about the others' names. They treated him like an animal in a cage. Samira was the only one who saw him as a person.

The small one with the wrinkled face, presumably Samira's servant, manipulated a mechanism of some kind, and scent after scent flooded into his cage. The more he experienced the memories of others, the more vividly his own past came back to him. He remembered Soft Meat and Distant Rain and Sharp Salt and the end of the world. Were they all dead? Or were they held in cages of their own? It seemed unlikely that the hairless mammals could have very many of these cages, but what did he know of their capabilities?

Then without warning, there came a memory of his own.

FIFTEEN DAYS UNTIL IMPACT.

The strain threatened to overwhelm him, as did the punishing schedule, working as a member of the telescope by night and to create the hibernation pits with Distant Rain during the day.

He worked side by side with her as dusk fell, hauling containers of test liquid around and doing whatever she told him, even if he didn't understand it. They worked directly in one of the pits now, not wanting to waste the time required to travel back and forth between the factory and the site.

Despite the pressure, Rain's enthusiasm for the work kept things positive. He wished he could have worked for her all these years instead of Sharp Salt. She was a much better leader, valuing his abilities and motivating him to succeed. She treated him like an equal instead of a servant.

Like a friend, even. They were both so tired it made them silly, cracking inappropriate jokes about the coming apocalypse even as they labored to survive it.

He would have to leave soon and return to the telescope yet again. He didn't know if he could stand another night standing in a field staring up at the sky, female domination or no. Eventually his body was just going to give out. Trying to survive the asteroid might kill him before the asteroid itself did.

In the growing darkness, he tripped over a spur of rock and sprawled right into Rain, knocking her flat. He struggled to get up, flooding her with scents of apology and embarrassment, but he tangled in her limbs, and fell flat again. Her scent overwhelmed him, and it was... amusement? She was laughing at him.

No, she was laughing with him. Her crazy, exhausted hilarity infected him, too, as his scents mingled with hers, no longer embarrassed but over-whelmed by the humor of it all. The pure ridiculousness of lying on top of each other in a pit, trying to save a civilization who wouldn't believe them, as extinction rained down from the sky.

Suddenly, there was another scent in the air. Prey realized how close his body was to hers. They were alone in the pit. Prey knew he wasn't much to look at, physically. He was small and drab even for a male. He had long ago given up visiting the breeding grounds, where females regu-larly overlooked him for more attractive choices, leaving him frustrated and ashamed.

But the scent coming from Rain made it clear what was on her mind. And there was no one else around.

Males rarely had any choices when it came to sex. Females ran society and chose whomever they liked, or fought with each other about mates without reference to the males themselves. Even in the act itself, the overwhelming domination of a female's sexual pheromones gave a male little option but to submit, just as they did in every other aspect of life.

As Rain's pheromones rushed over him, Prey gave himself over to the feeling. He pulled his body in close to hers, expecting her to take control of the experience. Almost as soon as they had started, though, the rush of pheromones stopped, drifting away into the night. Of course. She was regretting the impulse already. No one had ever actually wanted Prey. How could he have thought otherwise?

He was about to clamber up and apologize again, but she wrapped herself around him. She leaned her face in next to his so they were eye to eye.

Do you want this? *she sent.*

She was asking *him?*

More than survival, *he sent back.*

A wash of amusement from her spread over him, and then the pheromones began again, more gently this time. The scent prompted his response, but so subtly he knew he could have resisted if he wanted, could have run away and left her. He had never heard of such a thing. He threw himself into her embrace…

PREY LURCHED BACK into the present, mind reeling. *Rain!* The intimacy of the memory made him long for her. They had grown so close in those final days and weeks. All the dreams they had for how society could be different, the shared ideas for technology and scientific discovery. All of it lost.

It prompted a cascade in his mind, filling in all of the experiences and connections he had forgotten. He remembered the telescope and the asteroid and the hibernation chambers. He remembered the fighting at the end, and the many who didn't make it. They had intended to wake after only a few months. How long had it been? Were these hairless mammals from some other place in the cosmos? From Mars or Jupiter or one of the other bright objects in the sky? Had they come with the asteroid?

A thought struck him: What if the asteroid had not been a chunk of rock, as they had assumed, but a raft, specifically designed by creatures to travel between the planets as one might float from shore to shore across a lake? Had they come, then, on a mission of destruction? Had they killed his species to claim the Earth for themselves? Perhaps their own planet had become uninhabitable, or they just wished to expand and claim more for themselves. That would explain why he had awakened, not in the hibernation chamber, but in this prison.

Was there any hope in trying to defeat a species that could travel across the stars as easily as a lake, who could harness lightning and fashion a cage out of the very air? He had no idea how many of them there were or what weaknesses they had. Well, he did know they were made of flesh, and presumably they bled like any other animal. They looked easier to kill than most. But kill one, and the others could use their lightning on him. He might not even make it out of the cage.

But Samira treated him differently than the others. Maybe instead of waiting for them to make a mistake, he should try to communicate. She seemed to want to talk, and talking was the only way he would ever learn where he was and what had happened. At least then he would know what he was really up against.

He knew they communicated through sound, but their noises all sounded like grunts to him. He was learning to distinguish them a little and infer meaning, but with nothing to go on, it was very slow. As far as he could tell, they communicated thoughts in tiny, discrete pieces, with each noise symbolizing a single thing. It seemed a very limited way to communicate, because relationships among the objects and actions had to be inferred by adjacency, instead of mixing concepts together in smells to demonstrate how they related. It was a language without subtlety, trapped in a purely linear progression. Still, he wanted to learn.

HA-MEE-KAA! he said.

Samira shot to her feet. "Yes," she said, followed by a stream of sounds he couldn't decipher. "Yes," however, was a sound he recognized as indicating an affirmative.

EH, he tried. *YEH.*

He couldn't make the hissing sound at the end of the word. They held still, listening, but not understanding.

NE, he said. *YEH. NE. YEH.* He alternated shaking his head back and forth and bobbing up and down. Why couldn't they understand what he was doing? It was their language, after all.

Finally, Samira caught on. "No!" she shouted. "Yes! No, yes, no, yes."

YEH YEH YEH, Prey said.

The hairless mammals sprang into frantic action with a cascade of sounds he had no chance of deciphering. Samira waved her hands to silence them. She stood in front of Prey and pointed to the side of her head, where her ear was. "*Hear*," she said. "Can you *hear* me?"

YEH, Prey said.

She made more noises to the other mammals, and something happened to the sound coming through the mesh box at the top of his cage. Samira touched her ear again and moved her mouth in the same way as before, but this time no sound came out. He realized they had stopped whatever technology they used that transmitted the sound from her suit to his cage.

NE, he said.

Another explosion of excitement from the mammals as the sound from the box returned.

Finally, Prey thought. He moved as close as possible to the invisible barrier, turning his head sideways so that he could look Samira in the eye. He reached his own feathered arm to his face and pawed at his nostrils with one claw.

She watched him intently. She took a step forward and touched a finger to the front of her mask, pointing at her nose. "Smell," she said. "Can you smell me?"

NE, he said.

SAMIRA'S HEART thudded in her chest. She had just spoken, actually *spoken*, with an intelligent non-human. As far as she knew, it was the first time that had happened in the history of the world.

"You have to send him my scent," she said.

Alex frowned. "How would I even do that?" he said.

"Come on," she said. "He's asking to smell me. I've been sweating in this suit for hours; we just have to connect my suit to the pump."

"That would expose him to any bacteria that's in there with you," Paula said. "It would break our sterile environment, put him at risk of illness."

Samira slapped her hand against her suit in frustration. "He's the last of his species, and he's locked in a cage. He's trying to talk to us. We have to give him something."

"It's a risk," Paula said.

"Besides, it goes two ways," Alex said. "Remember, that thing's a killer, and it dominates its prey through scent."

"So make it one way," she said. The equipment they'd used to set up the pump was the same they used for the airflow in their suits. She was tired of precautions. It was the work of a moment to detach the air tube bringing fresh oxygen to her suit and connect it to the pump.

"Samira, stop. This is not a good idea," Alex said, but Paula held up a hand. "Let her go."

Samira ran the pump for just a second, then reconnected herself to the air. "It shouldn't take much," she said. "He's got the nose of a bloodhound."

"Sensors are picking up a lot of alkylpyrazines again," Alex said. "He's reacting."

Samira looked at Charlie and tapped the mask in front of her nose. "Can you *smell* me?" she asked.

Charlie met her gaze and squawked his bird-like cry. *YEH. YEH. YEH.*

CHAPTER TEN

Kit woke to chaos. He heard shouting, the slamming of doors, someone crying. He dressed quickly and ran out into the lobby of the hotel they had commandeered to serve as their headquarters in Chiang Rai.

Mai stalked through the lobby, her serene manner of the day before replaced with fury. She hurled orders in rapid Thai, sending aides and ministers rushing to do her bidding as more rushed in to answer her summons.

Arinya stood beside her, prioritizing the flow of people and keeping things organized. Kit made his way around the outside of the group, allowing himself to be seen without interrupting.

It didn't take long to understand what had happened. In a coordinated, surgical strike, an unknown group had raided their drug labs in both Thailand and Myanmar, destroying the equipment and stealing the domination chemical. All of it.

Kit's mind flew back to the CIA agent's visit. Had the Americans done this? They had sent special forces to take the chemical before. Balked in their attempts to strike a deal, they might have resorted to violence instead. Kit remembered the way he'd shouted at the American, perhaps not a wise approach when treating with a vastly superior power. Had he caused this? Should he have accepted American help instead of angering them?

It might not be the Americans, of course. General Wattana certainly knew that Mai was a threat to his power. She was all over social media and gave interviews to journalists, decrying his illegal coup and brutal murder of the royal family, accusing him of working for China, and calling all loyal Thai to flock to her banner. Even before the coup, she had been hugely popular for her activism and celebrity status as a young and beautiful princess. Now, as the only surviving heir of the Chakri dynasty who had upended the largest sex trafficking organization in Asia, she was beloved. Millions followed her online, and to the young women of Thailand, she was a national heroine. If Wattana could have assassinated her without turning her into a martyr, he probably would have done it.

Gradually, the room cleared, with instructions given to search the labs for evidence of who had perpetrated the attack, interview the guards (if any had survived), and above all, determine if any of the chemical remained. Only Arinya, Kit, and a doubled contingent of bodyguards remained behind.

"Come with me," Mai said. Arinya and Kit followed her into one of the hotel's conference rooms. "No one comes in," she told her bodyguards. Then she shut the door, leaving the three of them alone.

In a moment, the fiery activist disappeared and a frightened young woman appeared in her place. She collapsed into one of the faux leather swivel chairs, looking small and lost. As long as Kit had known Mai, her shell had never cracked. She was the Queen of Thailand, heir to a centuries-old dynasty, empowered by the will of her people and the righteousness of her cause. No one who met her doubted her confidence for a moment. Now she looked defeated. It rattled Kit to the bone.

"Your Majesty," he said.

Mai shook her head. "It's over. When you brought me that chemical, I knew we could use it to make a difference. And we did, at least for a short while." She laughed sadly. "We took over the largest crime syndicate in Asia in a matter of months! But it was already crumbling. We couldn't keep the men in line, not without a lot more of it. And now we have nothing."

"You are the queen," Kit protested. "The throne is yours by right."

"History is littered with the graves of rightful rulers who didn't have the power to hold their thrones," Mai said. "We didn't get this far because people believed in me. We got this far because we gave them no choice."

"The people love you," Kit said. "They want you, not Wattana."

Mai smiled wistfully. "Some vocal people on social media do, anyway," she said. "But our army doesn't. And that's what matters."

"What will you do?" Arinya asked.

"Exile is the best we can hope for. Cross back into Myanmar, then head for Europe, perhaps. There's nothing more we can do here."

Kit punched the table. "I won't accept that!"

Arinya glared at him, but Mai reached out and touched his hand. "Thank you for your loyalty," she said. "I release you from my service. Go to America, become a professor of paleontology. Follow your own dream, not mine."

Kit felt his eyes watering and angrily wiped away the tears. "*Thailand* is my dream. A strong Thailand without slavery or corruption where science can thrive. You can't give up. You can't."

"The world is afflicted by death and decay. But the wise do not grieve, having realized the nature of the world," Mai said. It was a Buddhist proverb.

Kit took her hands and held them tight, his gaze intent, and responded with a Buddhist proverb of his own. "Do today what must be done. Who knows? Tomorrow, death comes."

She smiled at him, radiant. "What would you have me do?"

Kit's mind raced. "March on Bangkok."

"Kit." He felt Arinya's hand on his shoulder, but he didn't look away from Mai.

"We can't," Arinya said. "Mai's right. The drug lords only follow her because of the chemical. The soldiers in our army are criminals; they might raid a town for money or the opportunity for violence, but they're not going to march against the army."

"Then leave them behind," Kit said. "Walk to Bangkok. Thailand will follow you."

"It's 800 kilometers to Bangkok," Arinya said. "It would take a month to walk there. Probably more."

"Start at Ayutthaya," Kit said, getting more excited. "The ancestral seat of the kings of Siam. Invite reporters. Tell them you're going home to reclaim your throne. Tell them you are following the way of peace. That you know your cause is right and you trust in the people of Thailand. Then actually start your walk at Wongwian Yai, by the statue of your great ancestor, across the Phra Phuttayotfa Bridge to the Grand Palace."

"Hey," Arinya grabbed his chin, forcing him to look at her. "Wattana killed her entire family. What makes you think he won't just kill her too?"

Kit turned back to Mai. It was easy to forget that behind the royal presence she generally displayed, she was a young woman whose family had been brutally murdered. "Conquer anger with non-anger," he said. "Conquer dishonesty with truth."

He saw the moment the spark relit in Mai's eyes. She nodded imperceptibly, then with growing enthusiasm.

"No," Arinya said. "Mai, this is crazy."

Mai stood, her back straight, and the old fire burned in her gaze. "Maybe crazy is all I have left."

THE DRIVE from Chiang Rai to Ayutthaya took ten hours. Halfway there, his back aching and his head pounding, the grand vision of that morning felt hard to hold onto. Kit hadn't considered all the practical obstacles to be overcome. It was easy to forget how big a place Thailand was.

The power base Mai had built for herself was mostly in the northern part of the country. It was there and across the border in Myanmar that the Red Wa primarily operated. The thousands of women Mai had freed, the organization she'd formed to help them reintegrate into society, the former drug runners that comprised her fragile army: all of that was in the Lanna region in the north. Moving even a fraction of those people to the south would be a huge operation involving an enormous number of vehicles, arrangements for food and housing, and a tremendous amount of money. It couldn't be done, not without Wattana knowing about it and interfering before they could even start.

As they had brought more of Mai's staff in on the plan and discussed the details, the whole scheme had started to unravel. Instead of a grand gesture of defiance, it had started to sound like a traveling circus. Wattana wouldn't even *need* to interfere; the whole plan would collapse under the weight of its own logistics.

So they just left. Mai selected three of her top aides and told them to do what they could to pave the way, then she walked out. Mongkut, a bodyguard who'd been with Mai since she was a little girl, joined them, and he, Mai, Arinya, and Kit set off in a Honda Civic, driving south on Route 1 toward the capital.

By the time they arrived, Mai's people had booked a hotel, and several reporters were waiting for them outside. Even though she had to be as exhausted from the drive as Kit, Mai didn't push past them, but stopped and spoke with them as energetically as if she'd just woken from a nap. She accused Wattana of murder and regicide and treason, called on all loyal Thais to throw off his rule, and told the reporters exactly what she planned to do.

"Aren't you afraid Wattana will kill you, too?" one of the reporters asked.

"If he wants to, let him do it," she said defiantly. "But he'll have to do it in the sunlight, with the eyes of every citizen on him. Tomorrow, we march."

Before she finished, several more cars of Red Wa body-guards arrived and took up places around the hotel. "Get some sleep," Mai said to Kit and Arinya.

KIT COULDN'T SLEEP. This had been his idea, but it was insane. She could be taken out by a sniper's bullet five minutes into the march. They could all be arrested and thrown into a dark hole, never to see the sun again. Wattana had the support of China; what did he care if he got some bad press?

Besides, he might not have to do anything. The whole scheme revolved around the assumption of Mai's popularity, that she would draw crowds and media coverage. What if no one came? Her grand march would be laughable, nothing more than a disaffected girl shouting insults at the palace from the street.

He lay in the unfamiliar bed, his fears running circles in his brain, keeping him from rest. He stared into the darkness, lit only by the thin red glow of the digital clock on the bedside table. He must have slept eventually, because morning came too fast, and with it a kind of resignation. Whatever came would come. Either they would die or be captured or… he couldn't quite imagine what it would look like if they succeeded. That probably wasn't a good sign.

He pulled on his clothes—the same ones he'd worn the day before—and went to join the others outside. More soldiers had arrived during the night, along with many of Mai's aides, advisors, and secretaries. They formed a caravan and drove toward Wongwian Yai.

At first, the early morning roads were clear, but as they approached the square—one of the busiest intersections in Bangkok—traffic snarled. Mai didn't wait. She climbed out of the car and started walking down the busy street.

"Wait," Kit said. "Princess!" But Mai didn't hear him or didn't choose to listen. Her coterie scrambled out of the other vehicles, abandoning them in the road, and rushed to catch up with her. Mongkut and the guards moved ahead, carving a path, and soon people started to recognize her. By the time they could see the statue of King Taksin up ahead, an excited crowd of people surged along behind them.

As they reached the square, they discovered the reason for the traffic jam. Wongwian Yai, usually a busy thoroughfare, was packed with people, completely blocking all the adjoining roads. The news of Mai's arrival lit through them like wildfire, drawing cheers and shouts. Many waved Mai's personal royal flag—purple for the day of her birth and emblazoned with the royal cypher and crown.

Mai herself wore a purple dress with a white sash and a pair of white sneakers. She spoke softly to Mongkut, who touched his ear and said something on his radio.

Mai walked alone toward the crowd. The guards stepped back, and at first, Kit feared the crowd would mob her. As she approached, though, they quieted and made room for her. Head high, she walked serenely into a corridor of people. Kit bit his lip. She was going to get herself killed.

Mai's coterie followed her through the gap. The guards, led by Mongkut, pushed in along the edges of the crowd, trying to widen the passage. Realizing he was about to be left behind, Kit dashed forward, just in time to stay with the group before the crowd closed around behind them. He pushed his way forward until he could at least see her. She walked with her eyes forward, barely acknowledging the people as they cheered and waved their flags and called her name. She was no pop star or beauty pageant contestant, to bask in their adulation. She was a queen, marching to reclaim her throne.

After several blocks, they managed to push through the gathered crowd and started up Prajadhipok Road toward downtown Bangkok. People thronged the overpass above them and threw down flowers. Cameras flashed and reporters scampered backwards, holding microphones at Mai, but she ignored them. It was a canny move, Kit thought. By not playing the game, she put herself above the fray. By not pushing her agenda, she drew the fascination of the country.

The crowd grew as they walked down the center of the multi-lane highway. The other roads into Wongwian Yai had been crammed with cars, but the way here was clear, kept that way by the sheer mass of people blocking the on-ramps, filling the road, and hanging from every overpass and building.

Helicopters roared overhead. Two news copters had already been covering the action from high in the air, but these new ones were military, and they dropped low enough that Kit could see their mounted guns and the soldiers on board. "You will clear the street," a man's voice boomed from a loudspeaker. "This is an unsanctioned gathering."

Mai kept walking, not even looking up.

"Clear the street, or you will be fired upon," the loudspeaker boomed.

Some of the crowd fell back, looking for cover, but many more pressed forward, gathering around Mai to protect her. The helicopters hovered menacingly, but did not actually open fire. The holiday mood in the crowd was gone, though, replaced with a sense of menace. This was no longer a victory parade.

That became more obvious when the march took the lower road toward the Memorial Bridge. The army was waiting for them. Military trucks barricaded the way ahead, filling the bridge, while rows of soldiers in riot gear stood across the road.

For the first time since leaving Wongwian Yai, Mai stopped. The crowd stopped with her, filling the space between the tall concrete barriers on both sides. Even if some of them had wanted to leave, they were hemmed in. There was nowhere to go. The soldiers held batons and shields and had rifles slung over their backs. Kit wondered if the guns were loaded with rubber bullets or live rounds.

Kit, standing right next to Arinya, saw her slip a vial from her pocket and empty it onto Mai's collar. "That's the last drop we have," she said quietly. "This had better work."

As the smell reached him, Kit felt his awe for Mai surge into deep loyalty and love. It didn't matter that he knew it was chemically induced. It didn't matter that he was already devoted to her. The chemical entered his mind, and he knew he would die for her, if she asked it.

Mai's voice rang clearly across the gap. "I am Somdet Phra Rajini Srinagarindra Chakri Sirindhorn. I am the rightful ruler of Thailand, heir to the Chakri Dynasty and your Queen." She walked forward, crossing the distance alone. The soldiers raised their shields, though what they thought they had to fear from an unarmed young woman, Kit had no idea.

Except, of course, that they did have something to fear.

She stopped six meters from their line. She looked from

one man to the next, waiting, Kit knew, for the smell of the domination chemical she wore to reach them. The Chinese had apparently not thought it worthwhile to share knowledge of the chemical with General Wattana, because the soldiers wore no gas masks.

Mai raised her voice again. "I command you to stand aside."

For a moment, Kit thought it wouldn't work. Then the soldiers lowered their shields and backed away to either side, making a path. Mai walked through.

With a shout of triumph, the crowd surged forward. Kit ran ahead, heedless of the danger, shouting, "Sirindhorn! Thailand!"

The soldiers threw down their weapons and joined the crowd, which surged across the bridge, scrambling over the barricades and vehicles. They danced past Wat Pho and through the Palace Park, their numbers growing as more and more people joined the march. In front of it all, Mai walked with calm purpose, almost as if she didn't notice that half of Bangkok had turned up to support her.

When they reached the palace complex, a crowd of a different kind waited for them. A tank blocked the street, and ranks of soldiers stood at attention. *This is where it happens*, Kit thought. *This is where the fantasy I sold her on shatters in blood and death.*

But he was wrong. On the steps a cluster of high-ranked officers stepped forward, their shirt fronts covered with ribbons and symbols of rank. They clasped their hands in a *wai* and held them high over their heads, bowing in the manner of respect for a monarch. Two soldiers stepped forward pushing a third man whose hands were cuffed behind his back. They forced him to his knees in front of the officers. It was General Wattana.

The general in the front of the group of officers drew his

pistol and held it to Wattana's head. The crowd went quiet. "Your Royal Majesty," the general called. "Say the word, and the traitor dies."

Mai took ten slow steps across the street, standing alone with the crowd at her back and the soldiers still ahead. A sergeant shouted something, and the ranks of soldiers saluted, hands snapping to their foreheads, followed by the rapid flick of the head to the left that was unique to the Thai military.

"The traitor dies," she said, in a voice that rang through the square.

A tiny part of Kit objected. This revolution had been entirely peaceful; why end it with blood now? But that part of himself was quickly overwhelmed by his feelings of devotion. The general fired, the noise a tiny pop over the noise of the crowd, and Wattana fell lifeless to the steps.

Mai turned and faced the crowd. "Today the people have spoken! Together we will cleanse the evil from our nation and build a strong and independent Thailand!"

The cheers of the crowd were deafening. He felt the surging force of the mass of people behind him, the energy that wanted to break out, thousands pushing to get closer to Mai and be a part of this momentous day. If they stampeded, the day could end in much more blood and death.

"Bow before your Queen!" Kit shouted. His voice was lost in the tumult. "Bow before your Queen!" he shouted again, and Arinya took up the cry. Kit threw himself to his knees and bent to the street, pressing his clasped hands to the pavement and his forehead to his hands. "Bow before your Queen!" he shouted again.

He thought he might just be trampled, but those near him saw and imitated his example. Thais knew to bow before royalty; the impulse was deep in their history and tradition. As soon as those behind saw the people in front of them fall to the ground, they dropped to their knees as well, until the entire square and those in the park and streets beyond were prostrate before Mai.

They had done it. She was queen.

CHAPTER ELEVEN

C harlie learned to speak with incredible speed.
Hundreds of bird species—distant relatives of maniraptors like Charlie—could mimic sounds with excellent precision, and not just other bird sounds, but slamming doors, car horns, water sprinklers, and, of course, human voices. The skill had independently evolved multiple times. The evolution of mimicry had always been driven by sexual selection, the female bird preferring the males with the most varied repertoire of songs.

Of course, Charlie wasn't just mimicking the sounds Samira made; he was understanding them. He was parsing the structure of the English language and learning how to put the pieces together to communicate thought. She couldn't imagine that in his place, surrounded by the squawking language that the males of his species used, she would have come close to such quick comprehension. It made her wonder if maniraptors were humanity's intellectual superiors.

They'd been practicing for weeks, and every day, he astounded her with his progress. He even learned to pronounce her name properly, though the 'S' came out a lot breathier than a human would do it. So far, their conversations had been restricted to practical, concrete things, mostly nouns she could communicate by pointing and verbs she could pantomime.

"Sa-mi-ra...eat...meat," Prey told her.

"Yes, I eat meat," she said. "I eat plants, too."

"Samira...eat...meat...today."

Samira looked at Paula. "I did eat a chicken sandwich in the cafeteria today. Is he asking me a question, or is he telling me?"

"No question," Prey said. "Telling."

Samira raised her eyebrows, once again startled by his quick understanding. "How do you know I ate meat today?"

"Smell meat."

She pointed to her mask. "No smell," she said. "Wear suit."

"Samira touch meat," he said. "Samira touch suit."

That couldn't be right, could it? His sense of smell couldn't be that good. Samira pointed at Paula. "Paula eat meat?"

"No. Paula eat plant."

"He's right," Paula said. "I had a salad."

"How is that possible? Do we have some kind of seal breach?" Samira looked back at Charlie. "Did I eat meat yesterday?"

"Not understand."

"Yesterday. Before sleep. Samira eat meat before sleep?"

"Different meat," Prey said.

"I had a ham sandwich yesterday," she said. "I think he really can smell it."

"What is...sandwich?" he asked.

"Sandwich is food. A kind of food. Food made from plants."

"Sandwich is plant food."

"Yes. Well, it's one kind of plant food, but we usually put

some kind of meat inside. It's...hard to explain. Don't worry about sandwiches."

"Not understand."

"Never mind. Don't worry about it."

"Not understand worry."

"Forget it. It's not important."

Prey snarled in frustration. Whenever he didn't understand something, he expressed his frustration in ways that might have sent her running for cover if there hadn't been a thick sheet of glass between them.

"Samira smell," Charlie said.

Now it was her turn not to understand. "Yes, I can smell. Not as well as you."

"No. Smell no suit."

She turned the phrase over in her head, trying to understand.

Charlie snarled again. "Samira no suit. Smell. Smell no suit."

Comprehension hit her. Of course. He was frustrated with struggling through this limited speech when he had a much easier way. "He wants me to smell him," Samira said. "He wants to communicate through scent, the way he would with his own kind."

"It's too dangerous," Paula said.

"I don't even have to go in there. I'll take off my helmet, and if I fall over, you can drag me out of here."

"He could kill you," Paula said. "He could dominate you and make you do something against your will."

"Do what? Open the cage? I don't even know how. Come on, it's low risk, and the risk is all to me. He just wants to send me a memory or a thought. He's made such an effort to learn to speak; the least we can do is let him communicate what he can in his own language."

Paula was silent for a long time. Finally, she nodded. "Okay. Under one condition. We tie you down."

"What?"

"I don't know what he could make you do. Hurt yourself. Kill me. We're not doing this unless I know we can do it safely."

Samira shrugged. "Whatever it takes."

Alex brought in a chair and some adjustable canvas straps used to tie equipment to dollies during transport. He strapped the back and rear legs of the chair to a support beam that held up the ceiling, and then strapped Samira into it at arms, legs, and waist.

"The things we do for science," she said. No one laughed. If Samira could have just pulled off her helmet immediately, she wouldn't have been so nervous about it, but all of this set up was increasing the suspense. She knew what it felt like for another person to have complete control over her choices, and it was horrible. Charlie was the source of those chemicals, with a lifetime of experience using them. What might he do to her mind?

"Okay," Alex said. "Are you ready?"

Samira nodded, not trusting her voice. With a tearing sound, Alex pulled away the Velcro that held her helmet seal in place and lifted the helmet off her head. The cool air struck her damp hair, and she involuntarily took a deep breath of fresh air. Without the suit's faceplate, the colors around her seemed brighter. She looked at Charlie, whose feathers, jaws, and teeth seemed closer and sharper than before.

He didn't waste any time. A rich aroma flooded the room. Samira jerked her head back, alarmed, afraid that Paula was right after all, and he was dominating her into submission. Then she saw the tyrannosaur.

It wasn't that she stopped seeing the room. It was more like her brain stopped paying attention to the input from her eyes, seeing the vision in her mind more brightly and clearly than the real world around her.

Despite only having seen fossils and artists' reconstructions, Samira recognized the creature in front of her as an Asian tyrannosaur, a Tarbosaurus, of which dozens of skeletons had been found in the Gobi Desert in Mongolia. This was no desert, though. It was a flooded plain of short vegetation, like a rice paddy, with river channels crossing through it. The tyrannosaur stood on a hill out of the water, perched on a rock like a giant, ungainly parrot.

A closer look told her that it really *was* a rice paddy, or something equivalent. This was *agriculture*, plants that had been intentionally cultivated. She quickly saw why—a herd of hadrosaurs, at least a hundred strong, lumbered through the water, chewing placidly on the vegetation. Three male maniraptors, responsible for pasturing the herd, cowered behind the beasts, afraid of the tyrannosaur. A lone female maniraptor—their leader—faced off against the predator, although it towered over her, outweighing her by tons.

As soon as Samira had processed the scene visually, the emotion of it washed over her, one of overwhelming terror. Not just the fear of bodily harm, but the fear of loss. Samira became Prey, the youngest and smallest of the males, and the female was his mother. He was only a child, learning the work under her dominance and guidance.

He squealed as his mother spread her feathers wide, trying to make herself appear larger to the giant predator. She flooded the air with scents to dominate the beast and send it away. It was rare that tyrannosaurs entered maniraptor territory at all. The borders were patrolled and regularly renewed with strong scents that warned predators away. Prey had never seen one before, nor heard of one coming near where maniraptors lived.

This one was huge, though, five tons at the least, and seemed unperturbed by the smells Prey's mother was creating. It opened massive jaws crammed with needle-sharp teeth, and the small part of her that still knew she was Samira was surprised when instead of a roar, it made a sharp screech. To

Prey, however, the noise was terrifying, and even his mother took a hop backwards before stopping again to hold her ground.

The tyrannosaur dipped its jaws toward her, but as it did, it caught a stronger dose of her scent. It paused and snorted, then scratched at its face, confused. Prey's view was partially blocked by the herd of hadrosaurs, but he saw her step forward, renewing her scent and trying to drive the tyrannosaur back.

It did retreat at first, whipping its giant head back and forth in confusion. Then its eyes focused on her, and without warning, it attacked, astonishingly agile for its bulk and—*like a bird, Samira thought*—landed claws-first on Prey's mother, pinioning her small body and driving its open mouth like a battering ram down on top of her. She died in an instant, crushed, and when the beast's head came up again, it tore half of her lifeless body away in its jaws.

Prey screamed. Samira felt the anguish of his loss tear through her, reliving his emotion as if it were her own. The other males scattered, but he stayed, unable to tear his eyes away. The hadrosaurs stayed as well, too stupid to run, or else intelligent enough to know that once the tyrannosaur had made a kill, it was no longer a threat. Prey watched in horror as the beast lowered its head for another grisly bite.

THE MEMORY CLEARED, and Samira found herself shaking in her chair, wracked with sobbing, her face running with tears. Alex and Paula crouched on either side of her, shaking her and calling her name. "I'm all right," she managed to say. She tried to lift her hands to her face, but they were still strapped down.

My name is Samira, she thought. *I'm a paleontologist. I'm human. That creature wasn't my mother, and she died sixty-six million years ago. She meant nothing to me.*

She still felt raw with grief. When she could catch her breath, she said in as calm a voice as she could manage, "I'm okay. It's done. Can you release me now?"

"Give it a moment," Paula said.

Samira lifted her head and looked at Prey—at Charlie. He looked back, his alien face unreadable. Why had he chosen that memory to show her? Was he trying to evoke her sympathy? She might have been angry at him for manipulating her emotions, but he had just communicated with her more fully and profoundly than with any of the English words he had learned. And whatever his intentions, she did sympathize with him.

More than his intelligence or the speed at which he had learned to speak, it was this direct experience of his consciousness that convinced her. This animal in the cage in front of her was a person. She'd known it intellectually before, but now it felt as real to her as it did when she thought of Paula or Alex or Beth. This sharing of memories was a closeness beyond anything she had experienced with any human, even her sister. A glimpse into the soul of another like what novels tried to do, but even the best of them gave only a poor reflection of reality. No human could touch another human mind like this.

She wondered if the experience had to be rendered truthfully, or if Charlie could embellish the memory, or even invent it from whole cloth. She believed it was a true story, but really, she didn't know. Its immersive detail seemed hard to fake, but she didn't know what he was capable of. Perhaps they told fiction as well, only crafted from scent and emotion. He was a person; she was certain of that. But how much could she trust him?

BACK IN PAULA'S office over a welcome cup of tea, Samira insisted that Beth be brought from her anatomy lab before she would tell them what she'd experienced. She'd been through an emotional ordeal, even if it wasn't hers, and felt a strong need to have her sister close by. When Beth arrived and sat next to her, Samira entwined a hand with hers and described what she had seen as thoroughly as she could, her voice hitching a few times with emotion at the memory. Shortly after she finished, Dan Everson joined them, and she explained it all over again.

"I think Charlie chose to share that because it was an emotional memory," Samira said. "He wasn't just passing information. He wants me to know him. To empathize with him about the death of his mother, which must have been a very significant moment in his life."

"And it worked," Paula said.

"Well, yeah. It was wonderful. I mean, it was awful, but the ability to directly experience what someone else is feeling? To actually become them for a time? We can never do that. Even close family members you've lived with for decades can only guess from outside cues. We can never know another human being, not the way Charlie's people know each other.

"We can speculate all we want about consciousness and self-awareness, but the only person I can really know about for sure is me. I assume you're self-aware because you act like me and talk like me. But Charlie wasn't just talking to me. He wasn't telling me a story; I was actually experiencing the event as he did. Or at least as he remembered it. I felt what he felt. There's no doubt that I was in a conscious and self-aware mind."

Beth asked some questions about anatomy, and Samira described the tyrannosaur and the hadrosaurs in as great a detail as possible. They agreed with her assessment that the tyrannosaur was a Tarbosaurus, consistent with recovered skeletons. Of particular interest was its skin, which had been a mottled gray, with a ragged plumage of thin, feathery strands at its throat. It was very rare to recover skin, hair, or feathers from any fossil, so what dinosaurs looked like on the outside was mostly a matter of guesswork.

The hadrosaurs, although similar in many ways to the known species Saurolophus, had a smaller and differently shaped crest, and they concluded it was probably a new species for which fossils had not yet been uncovered. This didn't surprise anyone, since of the estimated four thousand different dinosaur species that lived during the Mesozoic period, fewer than eight hundred had been found and named.

Samira, however, kept coming back to the experience itself. "I know there are people here working on the chemical Charlie uses to dominate his prey," she said. "But shouldn't we be trying to synthesize this, too? The ability to have other people experience our memories?"

Everson looked at her curiously. "Why? I mean sure, from a scientific perspective, you'd like to understand how it works. But you seem to mean more than that."

She looked at the others, astonished that they didn't understand. "This is what the world needs," she said. "Humans hate and fight one another because they stop believing those in another group are really people. If they could experience life as someone else, really *experience* it, then how could they hate? They would understand."

Everson frowned. "Seems a bit simplistic. People fight other people because they have something they want, or because they took something that used to be theirs. People want to gain power and keep power. That doesn't all disappear because I can experience someone else's memory."

"Sure, you're right," Samira said. "But it would go a long way, wouldn't it? Undermining prejudice, breaking down walls? Even in our own country: Imagine if white people could experience what it's like to live as an African-American? Not just be told about it, but remember facing prejudice, and actually feel it emotionally? What if a city Democrat could experience life as a rural Republican, or vice-versa? Wouldn't that make a lot of difference?"

"It might," Everson said, scratching at his short growth of beard. "And if we *did* go to war, something like that could go a long way towards undermining the enemy's will to fight. We could do a lot with that. Imagine propaganda that didn't just show pictures of civilian casualties, but made you actually *feel* it as if you were right there…"

"No," Samira said, appalled. "That's not what I'm saying at all. I'm saying we use it to *avoid* war."

"That's what I'm saying, too," Everson said.

"No, you're taking a tool for peace and plotting how to use it to make the other side lose!"

Paula reached toward the teapot that was nestled in a tea cozy on a side table. "Would anyone like another cup?"

Everson stood. "No, I think I've had enough."

"I haven't," Samira said. "Do you always run away from conversations when they get uncomfortable?"

Everson met her gaze, but took his time before responding. Samira held the look, not backing down.

"You worry me, doctor," he said. "You have a remarkably naive outlook on international politics, but you have academic connections in the Far East and a tendency to impulsive action. Not exactly a combination I value in a person read in to one the closest-held secrets of the United States government."

A chill ran through Samira. She knew Everson had the power to yank her security clearances and deny her access to Charlie, no matter how much Paula valued her contributions. She'd never been one to kiss up to authority, but she felt Beth's hand in hers, urging restraint, the same as she had in Thailand.

"You talk as if increasing our ability to win a war and trying to avoid one are different," Everson said. "But they're the *same thing*. It's called deterrence, and it's been at the center of U.S. military doctrine for over a century. China has three times our population; if we fought them on an even playing field, we'd lose. The only way we prevent conflict is by maintaining such technological superiority that no one dares to fight us. It might seem counterintuitive to you, but strengthening our military capability is how we keep the peace."

"And how we keep our power," she said.

Everson's fists clenched. "Yes," he said. "Of course, it's how we keep power. It's how we keep our wealth as a nation and maintain the systems around the world that provide us with the goods we value. And that wealth and freedom is what makes it possible, among other things, for us to invest in scientific exploration and fossil labs and send paleontologists around the world. I don't understand why you think I'm your enemy."

Samira stood, letting go of Beth's hand. She took a breath before opening her mouth. Controlling her voice felt like backing down to her, and she hated that. White men always thought they should get the last word, and it galled her to let him have it. Maybe the experience with Charlie was affecting her, though, because she could also see where he was coming from and recognize a thread of truth in it.

She sighed. "I don't think you're the enemy," she said. "I've seen what this technology can do, and it's scary. I don't trust our government to be quite as peace-loving as you seem to think, but I admit, we're not the ones invading other countries just because we want to control them. So I hope you're right. I hope we're the good guys. At any rate, I have no intention of spilling our secrets to the Chinese or Russians or anyone else." She held out her hand. "Friends?"

He hesitated for a moment, then took her hand and shook it briefly.

"I *would* like to study how these shared memories work,

though. I think it would be valuable to understand if they could be used to share human memories as well."

He narrowed her eyes at her, then nodded. "I'm okay with that," he said. "Subject to Paula's priorities as head of research."

She smiled. "Of course."

Everson nodded to Paula. "Thanks for the tea," he said, though he hadn't touched a drop. He strode out of the room.

"Whew," Beth said. "That could have gone worse. You're getting tactful in your old age."

Paula laughed. "That counts as tactful?"

"For Samira, it does."

"I was trying to imagine what I might see if I could use Charlie's method to share Everson's mind for a while," Samira said.

Beth smirked. "Learning diplomacy from a dinosaur?"

Samira nodded, serious. "We might learn a lot from him before this is over."

CHAPTER TWELVE

Afeter leaving Paula's office, Samira retreated to the facility's cafeteria, chose an uninspiring premade salad, and sat at a table by herself. Other people sat at the other tables, but she saw no one she knew. She wanted it that way. She needed to think.

Nobody else seemed to be grasping how revolutionary Charlie's ability could be. If humans could capture and share experiences that way, it could change everything. So much of the hatred in the world came from an inability to understand others. Leaders intentionally dehumanized other groups and painted them as dangerous to maintain their own power. Peace required compromise, and that only happened when people could understand each other across racial and cultural divides. Sure, those in power would want to stay in power, but they would no longer be able to dupe a populace into believing that the people on the other side of the river were baby-devouring barbarians. The populace would see that the others were different, but in many ways just like them.

She didn't even know if it was possible, of course. Charlie had evolved the ability to communicate that way; it didn't follow that scientists could figure out how to encode human experiences in the same way. But they ought to *try*. Experts in human cognition and brain chemistry should be brought in to attack the problem. Resources should be made available. If Everson wasn't interested, maybe she should go to Hunt and make her case.

But what if Everson was right? She knew that even if the technology were possible, it didn't mean that people would want the experience. After all, how many whites in the United States read books written by African Americans? The experience was available, but not many found it worth the trouble to understand. Not to mention the likelihood that some leaders or religious groups might ban the technology or pronounce it evil. People might consider it dangerous or disgusting to share the experiences of some hated group. And it hardly seemed right to force them.

She sighed. Maybe she was just letting her imagination get the best of her.

Two televisions mounted near the ceiling showed the news. A breathless field reporter in Nigeria described the newest outbreak of the Julian virus, with confirmed cases now in nineteen countries on five continents. More than ten thousand people had now lost their lives, almost half of them in Nigeria and Sierra Leone, where it had spread quickly, without sufficient medical infrastructure to detect and contain it. A single case in Charles de Gaulle airport in Paris was the only reported European incident to date, and had been quickly contained. That and the outbreak in Guadalajara, Mexico, however, had the American news media whipped into a panic that it might sweep across the United States at any moment.

The show switched to an interview with a virologist, who claimed the disease was baffling experts. "It's not like any virus we're familiar with," he said. "People hear 'virus' and they think COVID-19, but you have to understand, viruses are the most numerous biological entity on Earth. There are viruses as different from one another genetically as an elephant is from a tulip. They're as old as life itself, and they evolve rapidly. Julian is one of the largest viruses we've seen, with an extremely complex genome, and it can alter its shape to fit its environment. It not only infects humans, but we've found it in cows, dogs, cats, birds, and even many fish."

"Scary stuff," said the news anchor. "Some people think the US isn't doing enough to keep out the spread. We go now to Thailand, the first country to entirely close its borders to protect its citizens from the virus. Andrea, it sounds like the new regime is taking a bold stand. Should we be following suit before it's too late?"

The screen switched to a windblown reporter standing in front of an elaborate building that looked like it belonged in Venice instead of Bangkok. "Yes, it's true, Mark," she said in a British accent. "I'm standing here in front of Government House, where there have been many changes over the past year. Most Americans were evicted from the country a few months ago, but now they are allowing no foreigners to enter the country whatsoever, not even from China, who until recently exerted considerable influence on the government. The person who seems responsible for these changes is the newly crowned queen, Somdet Phra Rajini Sirindhorn."

"And that's quite a story in itself, isn't it, Andrea?"

"Yes, it is, Mark. Queen Sirindhorn's story involves an extraordinary quest to fight Thailand's sex trade and free young women from captivity. After the tragic deaths of the Thai royal family, her incredible journey has led her to be chosen as their new regent, a position she is taking quite seriously."

"To many, she's a heroine, a champion of women's rights who has accomplished more to stem the tide of human trafficking than many whole governments. But Andrea, how did she do it?"

The reporters kept talking, but Samira wasn't listening

anymore. She stood up, hardly realizing what she was doing. She stared at the television, where a photo of the new Thai queen now filled the screen. It wasn't the golden dress and sash or the silver crown that had caught her attention. It was the small man in a white military uniform standing behind her.

"I know him!" she said aloud. The other cafeteria-goers looked at her quizzically as the TV picture returned to the news anchor. "No, bring it back!" she said. She realized she was making a scene. "That was my friend. I *know* him."

This explanation didn't change the strange looks she was getting. "Sorry," she said. "I was just...excited to see a friend on TV." She sat down, mind racing. That was *Kit*. The last time she'd seen him, she'd been flying away in a helicopter, taking Charlie with her and leaving him behind. The soldiers had wired the site with explosives and detonated them once the helicopters were clear. She hadn't even known that Kit was still *alive*. And now here he was, standing behind the queen of Thailand. Had he been named to some high government office? Without her phone, she couldn't even look up more information.

She would have to get off site before she could investigate or send him a message, which she promised herself she would do that night. She wasn't hungry anymore. She dumped the rest of her salad in the trashcan and headed back to the lab.

SAMIRA NEVER WORE a hazmat suit in the lab anymore, even though the others still did. No one had forced the issue, so she was taking that for permission. For the past several days, she'd been trying to teach him English numbers. It was hard going after the first few. Because of the physical arrangement of their hands—three fingers and two opposing thumbs across from them—the maniraptors used a base-3 numbering system and an odd two-stage sequence for counting on their hands. It wasn't easy for Charlie to think in base-10, so understanding numbers required a lot of thought.

He'd been learning in spite of the challenge, and she was getting better at interpreting his finger/thumb arrangements as well. Today she'd been working on thousands, millions, and billions, trying to give him an intuitive sense for their meaning without having to do onerous mental calculations. By mid-afternoon, she thought he had it.

"How many humans there are?" Charlie asked. His pronunciation was still harsh, like a bird's squawk, but was getting more and more comprehensible each day.

"All together? It's getting close to ten billion now."

He made no change in posture or facial expression, but a light, sour smell like urine filled the air that she knew meant surprise.

"Billion?" he asked, pronouncing the 'b' precisely.

"Billion."

"On how many planets live?"

She laughed. "All on this one. On Earth."

"From where humans come?"

She hesitated. This was veering uncomfortably close to an explanation of what had happened to the rest of his species, a topic they hadn't decided how or when to broach. It was only recently that this conversation would even have been possible. Though she had to admit to herself that being able to explain those things was part of what motivated her to teach him big numbers. He deserved to know.

"Humans came from Earth," she said. "We've always been here."

His expression was unreadable. "How many year humans here?"

"About two hundred thousand years."

He considered the difficult number for a while. Then he asked, "How long my people not here?"

The simplicity of the question took her breath away. Just like that, he had leaped to the conclusion that his people were extinct.

She took a deep, careful breath and let it out again. "About sixty-six million years."

They stared at each other for a long time.

"I only one live," Charlie said.

"Yes." She wanted to reach through the glass and take his hand, stroke his feathers, anything to offer some small token of comfort. "You're the only one left."

A rush of scent filled the room. It brought no vision with it, but before she knew what was happening, there were tears on her face. Her legs gave way, and she slid to the floor, where she sat and wept, expressing sadness in the way of her species just as Charlie expressed it in the way of his.

CHAPTER THIRTEEN

K it's life had transformed beyond recognition. In just a few months, he'd gone from a minor university professor to one of the most powerful men in the country. Instead of fossil dust and lab equipment, he spent his days surrounded by larger-than-life portraits of Chakri kings, pillared balconies, statues of elephants, chandeliers, and ancestor shrines piled high with fresh flowers. Top government officials listened carefully to his opinions and enacted his programs to expand scientific investment. All because of Mai.

As far as he was concerned, she was more than just a queen. She was a goddess. Most people, given the power to force other people to do their bidding, would have used it selfishly, to make themselves rich or exact petty revenge. Mai had risked her own life, time and again, to rescue women from the trafficking trade and destroy the criminal industry that made it possible. She had even tracked down Arinya's sister, still alive in a Burmese military camp, and had brought her back to Thailand. Women across Southeast Asia worshiped Mai, and men did what she said whether they liked it or not.

The domination drug was gone. They'd used every gram they'd found, including what the Red Wa had stockpiled.

Fortunately, she barely needed it anymore. Her title and wealth and fame, along with the forcefulness of her personality, meant people obeyed her even without it. She had even abolished Thailand's long-standing *lèse majesté* laws that made it a crime to speak against the monarchy. Instead of increasing dissent, the move only seemed to solidify the populace's love for her as a modern queen of the people.

A small man dressed in the uniform of a palace chamberlain with a pink peony in his lapel approached Kit and bowed deeply with his hands pressed together. Kit didn't recognize him, but that wasn't surprising; the palace complex had lots of chamberlains. This one was ethnic Chinese, which made Kit guess he was from northern Thailand.

"The tailors are ready, General."

Kit cringed at the title, but Mai had insisted he needed a rank, as well as the clothes to go with it. The crimson brigadier general's uniform he'd been wearing in public was bad enough—he felt like an actor playing a part and felt sure the real military men around him resented him for wearing it. Today, however, Mai would be holding court in the throne room for a televised address, and she wanted him resplendent.

He followed the chamberlain through a series of high-ceilinged hallways wide enough to house whole families. The architecture of the palace had a strangely Western feel to it, having been commissioned by King Rama V after a visit to the capitals of Europe. Rama V, also known as Chulalongkorn, was the only Thai king that Americans had ever heard of, thanks to the seditious and fabricated journals of Anna Leonowens that had been popularized in the film *Anna and the King of Siam* and the musical *The King and I*. Both the musical and the film had long been banned in Thailand.

Three tailors waited for Kit with ludicrously embroidered articles of clothing draped over their arms. He submitted to their ministrations, standing on a stool and facing a full-length mirror with a lacquered teak wood frame. How had his life brought him to this? He was delighted to have Mai as queen. He was pleased with the chance to increase his nation's investment in the sciences. The honor was tremendous, but he didn't deserve it. He would have felt more at home as a simple professor again, fielding expeditions and teaching classes at the university.

As the tailors threaded his arms into a gold sequin-encrusted uniform jacket, Kit watched CNN on a television set mounted above the mirror. So much of the news revolved around the Julian virus these days. At Kit's recommendation, Mai had closed the country to all foreigners, and no cases had yet surfaced in Thailand. They'd needed to shut out foreign influence anyway, especially the Chinese, in order to consolidate their power. The virus gave them an excuse.

THOROUGHLY DRESSED AND DECORATED, Kit followed the chamberlain to the throne hall, a spectacular series of domes as high and stunningly painted as any Western cathedral. Mammoth marble pillars and intricately worked arches soared over murals depicting the exploits of the Chakri Dynasty kings. At the end of a long crimson carpet, a sun-dappled Buddha statue hovered over a tiered, golden throne.

Kit stepped out of his shoes and walked barefoot across the thick carpet. Mai stood on the dais in front of the throne, magnificent in her royal regalia. Her gown glittered with a fractal gold filigree that somehow drew all eyes to her despite the brilliance of the room. Several TV crews set up their cameras and lights behind pillars on each side, looking as crudely out of place as cockroaches on a wedding cake.

Kit stopped. Something was wrong. Not the TV people; they ruined the aesthetic, but they were supposed to be there. The usual crowd of courtiers, advisors, secretaries, and bodyguards filled the room, enough people that Kit couldn't at first identify what seemed so out of place. Arinya stood at the queen's side, looking calm and unconcerned. She was Thanpuying Arinya Tavaranan now, with an aristocratic title and an elegant red dress trimmed with gold to go with it.

Then he saw them: six men of Chinese ancestry standing unobtrusively around the room in the uniforms of palace chamberlains, all of them with peonies in their lapels. He didn't recognize any of them. Just one that he didn't recognize wasn't surprising. But six? And all of them Chinese?

Then he saw one he *did* recognize, standing in the back, his bald head glinting in the harsh lights of the TV crew. It was unmistakably the colonel, the same man who had forced Kit and Arinya to work for him to extract the chemical from the dig site in Khai Nun. The man Kit had prevented Arinya from killing after the explosion that destroyed the remaining fossils. The palace uniform couldn't disguise his gaunt face and sour expression. Kit's muscles clenched and he took a step backward, intending to sneak out before he was noticed.

"Keep walking and say nothing." The chamberlain he had come in with spoke calmly in his ear. Kit caught only the faintest whiff of that sweet petroleum smell he'd come to know so well. He knew exactly what it was, but it was too late.

Kit tried to turn and escape, but as soon as the thought came to him, he lost the will to try. What was the point in resisting? They were beaten. Knowing that the feeling came from the chemical he was breathing didn't stop him from feeling it. Helpless, he walked forward as instructed and took his place behind the throne. He cursed himself silently. Had they gotten to Mai? Of course they had. She smiled and stood tall, but her face was unnaturally pale. She must be furious on the inside, but with no choice but to obey.

He'd been so stupid! Her ascension to the throne had gone so smoothly, with so little actual resistance, that he'd been lulled into a feeling of inevitability. But they had *known* the Chinese had the domination drug. How had they imagined that security checks at the airports would stop them from coming?

It quickly became clear that not only did the Chinese know how to dominate with the drug, they were skilled at doing so discreetly. They controlled the proceedings with subtlety, never drawing overt attention to themselves. Most of the attendees probably looked right past them. How many more of them were there? How many people in this palace or throughout the government took their orders from Beijing?

The TV crews started filming as the rituals of prayers and lit candles were observed. Kit stood next to Mai, wanting to scream. They were going to replace her on the throne, or else turn her into a puppet, and there was nothing Kit could do about it. He couldn't speak or even move from the place he'd been instructed to stand.

Any hope Kit had that Mai had somehow resisted their attack vanished when she spoke. "I am honored by the love and support with which the Thai people have welcomed me. Many have asked when I will take a husband. I am now pleased to announce my engagement to Zhang Hai, the son of the Chairman of the Central Military Commission of the People's Republic of China." She held out a graceful hand. A young man wearing a white suit with a peony in his lapel stepped out of the crowd and took it. She smiled warmly at him and held up his hand between them. "May the love we have for each other represent the love that the great countries of China and Thailand hold for each other. May our personal union begin a new era of cooperation and friendship with our big brother China as equals and allies."

Kit groaned inwardly. It was a prepared speech, one she had clearly been forced to recite. Had she even met Zhang Hai before today? The Chinese chamberlain told Kit to smile and applaud, and so he did. Everyone applauded as the cameras swept the room. How many of them did so willingly, in ignorance of the coup, and how many because they were under the sway of the Chinese?

He gritted his teeth through his smile. For weeks now, he and Mai and Arinya had dominated others into doing their will, and only now did he remember what it felt like to be in someone else's control. How could he have been so foolish? The Chinese had talked their way through security as easily as Mai had done to the Red Wa in Tachileik. But it was too late to fix it now. There was no going back.

The peony in the chamberlain's lapel reeked; clearly it was the source of the domination chemical. At some level, deep in his mind, Kit wanted to snatch it from him, but when it came to actually doing so, he was completely incapable. He was under the man's sway, which meant submitting to his desires, even without explicit instructions. The Chinese spy hadn't specifically commanded Kit not to steal his flower, but he was still too under his control to bring himself to do it.

The press conference over, bodyguards surrounded Mai, blocking her from view. The Chinese took control. Quietly, they moved through the crowd, murmuring for people to step back. The colonel put a hand on Mai's shoulder, and before Kit could do anything about it, her bodyguards had whisked her away, with the Chinese following close behind.

Kit caught a glimpse of her, arm in arm with Zhang Hai, as they exited the throne room. He wondered if he'd ever see her again.

CHAPTER FOURTEEN

She found Paula in her office and told her about her conversation with Charlie.

"You told him he was the only one left?"

"I had to. He pretty much asked me directly." She didn't mention that she had specifically taught him the vocabulary needed to ask the question.

Paula tapped a pen on her desk. "I would have preferred to keep that from him as long as possible, but I guess it can't be helped. I hope it doesn't affect him too profoundly. I don't want him slipping into a depression and not eating or anything."

"Honestly, I think he had already guessed. Though the length of time surprised him. He didn't understand we were natives here. He thought we were aliens from another planet."

"Huh. I guess that's a logical guess, from his perspective. It's what I'd guess if I woke up surrounded by intelligent creatures I'd never seen before with technology I never thought possible."

Samira also told Paula about seeing Kit on the news. "I'm going to head out early and try to contact him," she said. "I've been here late so many nights anyway; it would be good to spend some time with Beth and Wallace."

"Go," Paula said, barely looking up from her computer screen. "Though anything you get out of your Thai friend seems like information Everson would be interested in."

Samira made a face. "Yes, I guess he would. Sorry for making a scene in here with him. Are you doing okay?"

"Yes, yes," Paula said, waving away her concern. "I'm doing fine. Frustrated, but fine. I'm trying to understand how these hibernation chambers could have worked. Did you know that there are frogs that freeze solid every winter? Their hearts stop beating, their blood doesn't flow, their cells can't communicate with each other. For all practical purposes, they're dead, but when spring comes, they thaw and hop away."

"Maniraptors don't hibernate, though," Samira said.

"No, it's not a natural ability. It must have been technological, and it must have been an extraordinary technology to have preserved life for so long. I've been studying the muck we found Charlie encased in, and it has some incredible insulation properties, among other things. But the very fact that Charlie's here suggests that life itself isn't dependent on motion or heat or a continuous source of energy to persist, because he would have had none of those things. The technology doesn't seem dependent on raptor physiology at all. Which suggests that, if we knew how to do it, we could freeze a *human being* solid and then bring them back to life again."

Samira tapped her lip. "It doesn't make sense to me."

"What, that life can be that resilient?"

"No, what I don't understand is their level of technology. From everything we've seen in their memories, this is a pre-industrial society. There are no cities, no factories, no vehicles, no burning of fossil fuels. They farm and herd animals, but not much more. How could a civilization like that develop a biomedical technology so much superior to ours?"

"They had more technology than you think," Paula said.

"I've been studying those memories longer than you have. Did you notice that music-making device?"

Samira considered. "I vaguely remember something like that."

"It was ordinary for them, so they didn't pay much attention to it. But it was an organic device—a living machine. It wasn't anything that evolved naturally. They grew it somehow, or genetically modified another organism to create it. Think of the Ductwork—I think that was organic as well, or had organic parts. I've been hoping to uncover some kind of memory of how such things were made, but so far, they've only appeared on the outskirts."

"So you think tech development can take more than one path. That maybe they didn't discover iron smelting or electricity, but they discovered ways to play with genetics that we've never even considered."

"I think their tech is driven by their physical biology, just like their numbering system is," Paula said. "What we discover or invent is affected by what we need or what we're looking for. Their communication through the sense of smell meant they needed to store and recreate smells, which may have pushed them toward an earlier understanding of chemistry and biology. Their physical bodies, their place in the food chain, what they needed to survive: all of that drove them down a different technological path, one unrecognizable to us."

"I could ask Charlie," Samira said. "He's getting a lot better at speaking, and he's incredibly smart. I bet he'd understand what I was asking."

"I was hoping you'd say that."

"I have a feeling we're going to be learning new things from Charlie for a long time," Samira said.

Paula gave a short laugh. "No kidding."

"Which is why we should have the whole world working on it."

Paula closed her eyes and sighed. "I know your feelings on that already. Now go home. Give Wallace a peanut butter cracker for me."

"I'll do that," Samira said.

FOR ONCE, Samira was ready to leave the facility before Beth. She waited while Beth wrote a few more lines of code in *R*. What was the deal with naming computer languages after single letters, anyway? Samira had never been much good at programming, but Beth had taken to it in grad school. She could process huge amounts of data and spit out graphs and statistical insights that would have taken Samira hours of fighting with Excel.

When she finished, they drove back to their apartment. With Beth at the wheel, Samira watched the world slide by out the passenger window, a rare view of sunlight.

"I keep asking myself if I'm doing the right thing," Samira said. "Charlie's basically a prisoner there. It's wrong. He should be in a wide-open space somewhere, able to live his life the way he chooses. This is basically Area 51, and we're the people hiding the aliens."

"I know, Sami. We've been over and over this. There's nothing you can do about it."

"I could tell people."

"Then you'd be in jail, and Charlie would still be in the same place. And even if you could get him out and everyone knew, it might not make his life better. Instead of just being used by the CIA, there would be a big fight over who gets to use him. He still wouldn't be left alone to make his own choices. You can't fix this, Samira."

Samira slumped further down in her seat. "I know. I just can't be okay with it."

The moment they walked into their apartment, Wallace

began squawking for attention. With all the hours she worked, he wasn't getting the love he needed, which made Samira feel guilty. She was feeling guilty about a lot of things lately, which she hated. She'd much rather feel angry. Give her a good fight any day over this helpless inaction.

She scratched Wallace's neck, reaching under the feathers, and nuzzled him affectionately. She gave him a peanut butter cracker. "That's from Paula," she said.

After Wallace was settled, she pulled out her phone and found Kit's number. Speaking of feeling guilty. How could she not have tried to call Kit before this, at least to see if he was still alive? The answer, of course, was that she hadn't wanted to know. It had been bad enough to be part of a military raid that had stolen fossils right out from under his nose. She hadn't wanted to think about the possibility that the raid had also killed her friend. The best case was that he would be alive and simply hate her for what she'd done. So she hadn't called.

She stared at his number for a long time, trying to work up the nerve.

"Just do it," Beth said. "Stop torturing yourself."

Samira held out the phone. "You want to make the call?"

"Not really."

"Fine." She huffed out a breath. "Here goes nothing."

She pressed the button and held the phone up to her ear. She heard a staticky ring, then another, and another. She counted to ten. No answer. She hung up the phone, feeling a combined sense of relief that he hadn't answered and annoyance that the task was now still hanging over her.

Instead, she searched the internet, looking for news about Thailand. She found a lot of stuff about the new queen, a longtime activist against sex trafficking who had risen to power on a wave of popular affection. Despite her time in Thailand, Samira still had trouble understanding Thai politics. How much power did the royal family actually have compared to the military or the national assembly? It had been a military coup that had thrown them out of Thailand, but now Queen Sirindhorn had taken control, apparently with the support of a major crime syndicate. Which didn't make much sense for an anti-crime activist. It was all so confusing.

She also found news about the queen's engagement to a young Chinese man, the son of one of the top leaders in the PRC. Samira guessed that wasn't good news for Everson and his friends in the CIA, but the internet seemed much more interested in whether he was cute enough for her, what she would wear at their wedding, and why he was so fond of wearing pink flowers in his lapels. Samira didn't care about any of that. She wanted to know about Kit.

She found very little. She found him in the background of a few pictures, and one paragraph toward the bottom of an article mentioned that he'd been named Science Minister. Good for him. He'd always wanted to expand the role of science in his country. Maybe now he could make those dreams come true.

Maybe he'd even forgive her for invading his country with American special forces, stealing his fossils, and blowing up their dig site. Though when she put it that way, probably not.

Sighing, she punched his name on her cell phone and tried to call him one last time.

CHAPTER FIFTEEN

Kit ran. No one stopped him as he fled the palace grounds. Either the Chinese didn't control enough of the palace security yet, or despite his newly-minted rank, he was of no consequence. Neither powerful enough to imprison or kill, nor useful enough to enslave. He hadn't seen Arinya again since she had disappeared behind closed doors with the queen, and he feared she was also captured and controlled, if not dead.

Out in the streets of Bangkok, he kept running, losing himself in the maze of the capital before anyone could notice he was gone and come after him. He wandered, anonymous in the crowds, relishing the aromas of motorcycle exhaust, fish sauce, and curry. Anything that didn't smell like sweet petroleum.

Lines of street vendor carts selling meat skewers and noodle dishes of all varieties crowded the sidewalks, forcing foot traffic into a narrow walkway against the curb. He nearly tripped over a man with no legs lying prone on the pavement, banging a tin cup for alms. Kit poured a handful of ten-baht coins into the cup, even though he knew the money would likely go to the mafia who ran most of the city's beggars.

Perhaps with a little more time, Mai could have overturned the city's organized crime as effectively as she had done with the Red Wa. Now they would never know.

A sharp smell set his pulse racing, but it was just a vendor cutting durian into slices to sell. He stalked on, no destination in mind. He felt like a coward. He had abandoned Mai and Arinya to little better than slavery. The thought gnawed at him. But what could he do about it? He had no more of the domination drug and no way to get it. He had no powerful friends, no influence. At this point, the best he could hope for was that the Americans would realize what was going on and force the Chinese to back off. He didn't love the Americans any more than the Chinese, but sometimes the only way to fight a snake was with a bigger snake.

He had a little money in the bank, which he used to rent a tiny apartment in one of Bangkok's many concrete block towers. He had no job and nothing to do, but he couldn't just slink back to Nakhon Ratchasima as if nothing had ever happened, leaving Mai and Arinya to their fate. He took to hanging around outside the white wall that surrounded the palace grounds, watching people come and go, though of course he never saw Mai except on television.

She appeared regularly, beautiful in her queenly regalia, as elegant and composed as if she'd been born to the role. She never spoke plainly about Thailand's problems, though, as she had done before. Instead, she delivered grand speeches that mostly praised Chinese actions and the benefits of a close alliance with China, their "big brother" on the world stage. They were transparently written for her, and even people who knew nothing about the domination drug must know she was a Chinese puppet.

A week later, the president of Taiwan got on international television and publicly invited China to enter the country and repatriate "Taiwan province," despite having run on an anti-China election campaign. He told the American carrier group in the Taiwan Strait to leave their waters and not interfere. "The right hand of China has for too long been cut off," he said. "It is the will of Taiwan that we be a unified China once again, in truth as well as name." The news cut to riots in the streets of Taipei.

Kit watched, dumbly astonished but not really surprised. At this rate, China would control all of Southeast Asia and the western Pacific by year's end. Perhaps they already did control it. Would Japan go next? All they had to do to conquer it was walk into Tokyo and start talking.

But where were they getting so much of the drug? Had they really found enough fossil locations to extract the liquid to maintain control of whole countries? He supposed it didn't necessarily take much—the Taiwanese president's invitation would be enough to send the PRC military, and probably muddied the diplomatic waters enough that the United States wouldn't be able to intervene without an international backlash. But Mai had run out of their stores just trying to control a single country.

Kit bought a package of cotton balls from a drugstore and started wearing them stuffed in his nose. It was uncomfortable, and it made his tongue dry out from breathing only through his mouth, but it was worth it for the knowledge that he couldn't be swayed.

He wondered how long it would be before someone noticed him loitering outside the palace every day, hiding among the tourists. There weren't many tourists these days, with the airports still closed to foreigners for fear of the Julian virus. He took pictures with his phone like a tourist, but he took them of the people who went in and out and the license plates of the cars they drove. Suspicious behavior, if anyone was watching. Perhaps they did notice him but just didn't consider him much of a threat.

The truth was, he wasn't a threat. He scoured the pictures in his bare apartment at night, looking for the Chinese and learning their faces. It wasn't easy to distinguish Thai citizens of Chinese ancestry from the Chinese agents themselves, but with enough online research, he could usually identify most of them.

But who was he kidding? Was he going to storm the palace and demand Mai's release? Champion a resistance movement and organize a sting operation? Set up a sniper's nest in a nearby building and pick off Chinese agents as they stepped out? It was ridiculous. He was powerless. He was only keeping busy to fool himself into thinking there was something he could do.

Just as he was about to leave for the day and go find some food, he spotted the colonel himself leaving on foot by a side gate. Kit hadn't seen the man since that day in the throne room, but after a lot of research—mostly paging through old Chinese military enlistment records online—he had identified him. He really was a colonel, but in the People's Liberation Army of China, not the Royal Thai Army. Colonel Feng Zhanwei had insinuated himself into the Thai armed forces, probably through old-fashioned tradecraft instead of chemical domination, or perhaps with the complicity of high-ranking Thais in the old regime.

Kit followed him. Zhanwei wore civilian clothes, a simple black suit that any of a million Bangkok businessmen would be wearing in the streets at this time of day, though he wore a fresh peony in his lapel. The colonel walked confidently down the tree-lined Ratchadamnoen Nok avenue, past flowered shrines with Mai's face on them, heading south by the ministry buildings. He turned left onto Chakkraphat, past rows of homes and shops with dozens of tangled electrical wires crisscrossing each other overhead.

Kit thought he might be heading for a rice shop or for some coffee, but he kept going, crossing the Phanfa Bridge. He passed several elevated train platforms, but didn't even look at them. The weather was pleasant, the heat dissipating as the sun grew low in the sky, so perhaps he was just enjoying the walk. Finally, his destination became clear: Sampeng Lane market in Chinatown. At this time of day, the narrow, winding paths were choked with people jostling each other to squeeze between stalls overflowing with hot cooked food.

As Zhanwei made his way through the tight-packed market, however, the crowd parted to let him pass. No one looked at him or paid him any attention, but they nevertheless scrambled to let him through. Kit wondered if he was telling them to move out of the way, or if the smell from the peony was enough to make them step aside. With cotton stuffed up his nose, Kit couldn't smell anything, not the domination drug or the spicy food sizzling in carts and folding tables on every side.

Zhanwei sampled the food as he walked, and no one objected or asked him to pay. At one point, a pretty young woman walked past, holding hands with a young man. Zhanwei said something to the girl, and she put her arms around Zhanwei's neck and kissed him gently on the mouth. Her boyfriend said nothing. Zhanwei smiled, patted her back-side, and walked on.

Kit wanted to throw up. If he behaved like this on the street, what was he doing to Mai and Arinya? Kit picked up his pace, closing in on the colonel while he perused a selection of dishes from a smiling vendor. Zhanwei chose a seafood dish and took it without paying. Kit growled. The man had the whole treasury of Thailand at his disposal, could get any food he wanted prepared expertly for him by palace chefs, but he couldn't pay a poor street vendor a few lousy baht?

Zhanwei sidled into a nook where a noodle shop owner had squeezed a few chairs and a table under a metal awning. A family had been there eating guay diow, but they cleared out when Zhanwei waved them away. He settled into one of the chairs and dug chopsticks into his fish.

Kit couldn't stand it anymore. He didn't have a plan; he

just acted. While Zhanwei was focused on his meal, Kit charged up behind him and attacked. With one hand, he snatched the peony from the colonel's lapel, and with the other he pulled the plug out of Zhanwei's nose. Before he could react, Kit kicked him away hard enough that the plastic chair buckled and collapsed, sending him sprawling into the street.

Kit tucked the peony into his own shirt pocket and threw the man's noseplug aside. The cotton in his own nose prevented him from smelling the flower, but he didn't need to smell it to know what it was. Zhanwei, realizing immediately what was happening, scrambled to his feet and took off through the crowd.

Kit ran after him, plowing through the people so they would smell the scent flooding from his peony and know it came from him. "That man stole my wallet!" he shouted. "Stop him!"

The market crowd reacted, cutting off Zhanwei's escape and holding him fast. Kit felt the exhilaration of commanding the obedience of others. This was power. He could do anything he wanted.

But no. He could do anything he wanted until he ran out of chemical, and then he would have to face the consequences. Besides, there was only one thing he wanted.

The crowd parted as he walked toward Zhanwei, who cowered and held his nose tightly shut.

"Pull his hands away from his face," Kit said.

Two men on either side of the colonel did.

"Keep your airways clear," Kit said. "Don't touch me or take anything from me. Come with me."

Zhanwei stood up and followed him.

The next problem was where to go. First, he found the seafood vendor and told Zhanwei to pay for the meal. When Zhanwei pulled out a sheaf of bills, Kit told him to give him triple what the meal was worth. He spotted a leather goods shop stuffed with knockoff Gucci and Prada wallets and purses. The shop was just a concrete room with a metal garage door that rolled down from above. Kit told the shopkeeper to leave and had Zhanwei pay him handsomely for the trouble. Then Kit rolled down the door with only the two of them inside.

Two dim electric bulbs lit the tiny space. The air turned hot and stale.

"Where is the princess? What are you doing to her?" Kit demanded.

The man cringed, his bald head beading with sweat. "She is safe, I swear it. She is treated well."

"And you force her to make the decisions you want?"

"Yes. We control the whole government now. There will be no more petty feuding. All will be united under China, as is only right and good." The man spoke with the fervor of a zealot.

"What about Arinya Tavaranan? Is she safe as well?"

"She serves the princess. She does as we tell her."

"What is your plan? What comes next?"

"Next? All of the world, of course. All the people of Earth will finally live in peace. We will no longer squander our resources on wars no one can win. Only when humanity is united will we be free to build our future, explore the stars, conquer our own genomes. This is the beginning of everything."

"You idiot," Kit said. "This drug will cause the biggest war in history. Everyone will fight to control it. Your glorious future is only wonderful for the ones pulling the strings. No one wants peace at the cost of their own slavery. How do you like it now that I'm in charge?"

"You used the drug to rule Thailand before we ever came," Zhanwei pointed out.

Kit winced, because of course he was right. Mai insisted

they were using it for good, and Kit still thought they had been. But Zhanwei thought the same thing.

"I wish you to let me go," Zhanwei said.

"Of course you do. But not until you answer my questions. How many Chinese agents

are using the drug in Thailand?"

"Twenty here in Bangkok."

The way he said it gave Kit pause. "And elsewhere in Thailand?"

"My men are all here. But the Ministry of State Security has their own agents who do not answer to me. It was they who supplied the Red Wa, and at one point had a presence in Chiang Mai. Princess Sirindhorn destroyed much of their influence in that region, though, so I don't know if any remain."

"You think you can unify the world, but you already have factions even in your own country," Kit said. "The more knowledge of the drug spreads, the worse it will get. People will never stop fighting for it."

"China is the greatest nation on Earth," Zhanwei said. "We have unified our vast region with its many languages and cultures, and we can bring that same peace to the world."

"I saw the news about Taiwan. Are you taking over other countries as well?"

"Taiwan has always been ours," the colonel snapped. "But yes, we have men with the drug in Hanoi, Tokyo, Seoul, Pyongyang, Jakarta, Manila. None in New Delhi yet, but that will come soon." He spoke with pride. "And of course, we have a few men in the halls of power of Washington, D.C."

"How can you possibly supply so many agents with the drug?" Kit asked. He and Arinya had confiscated all of the Red Wa's supply—which had also come from China—but they had run through it quickly. Only tiny amounts had come from the fossil site. "How much do you have? How many fossils have you found?"

Zhanwei chuckled. "If you were not forcing my truthfulness, you would not believe me."

"Tell me."

"It is not from the dead dinosaurs. It is from a living one."

Kit stared, uncertain how to take this. "No riddles," he said. "Tell me what you mean."

"I mean what I said. A living dinosaur, with scent glands from which this marvelous and miraculous substance is extracted."

"A dinosaur. You mean a modern bird? Speak plainly!"

The colonel cringed, the scent making him docile, eager to please. "I am speaking plainly; you do not believe me. A genuine dinosaur, a maniraptor, one who lived during the Cretaceous period and was preserved through means I do not understand, resides now, very much alive, in a special protected facility made from a large cave in Yunnan province."

"Impossible. You've seen it?"

"With my own eyes."

Kit narrowed his eyes at the man, but he seemed sincere. "Describe it."

"It does look rather like a bird. Talons, feathers, a tail. The feathers are vanes with little tufts, not like flying feathers, and it has a jaw filled with teeth instead of a beak. And hands. Hands like a chameleon's, with two thumbs, that can grasp and throw and manipulate objects as easily as any human."

"How big is it?"

"Big. Two meters tall at least, and twice the weight of a man."

A female, then. Zhanwei's description matched the maniraptors Kit had seen in the chemical-induced visions. "You're sure what you saw wasn't a hallucination? The drug—"

"I know what the drug does. This creature bit a soldier's hand off. Does that sound like a hallucination to you?"

"No."

"The soldier didn't think so either, at least judging by how he was screaming. Besides, hallucinations aren't a source of chemicals. This dinosaur is."

Amazing. It seemed impossible, but Kit remembered the hibernation chamber from the vision Arinya had told him. He remembered scrambling into a nest on the platform as earthquakes from the asteroid strike shook the ravine. Had a maniraptor really survived in stasis all this time? It certainly would explain where the Chinese were getting such a continuous supply of the drug.

He made Zhanwei give him all the details of Mai's schedule and where she was being held. Now he just had to figure out how to use Zhanwei to get in and get Mai and Arinya out.

"How long will it be until you're missed at the palace and someone comes looking for you?"

"They already are looking," Zhanwei said. "We have training for this kind of situation. When I ran away from you into the crowd, I signaled them that I was under duress. They will be here any moment."

Kit jumped to his feet. The leather goods shop was a trap, with only one way out. He should have known it was too easy. "Follow me," he said.

He rolled up the door and raced out. There were soldiers everywhere. They wore gas masks and probed into every corner of the market. Much of the foot traffic was gone. Shouts rang out as soon as he was seen. He zigged and zagged his way around stalls, the colonel right behind him. Zhanwei was older, though, and not accustomed to running. He fell quickly behind, and Kit couldn't afford to slow down. Compelled to follow, Zhanwei pushed his body to keep up, but his legs betrayed him, and he fell.

Kit lost himself in the twisted roads of Bangkok, changing direction as often as possible. When he spotted the orange vest of a motorbike taxi driver, he hopped aboard, and soon they were darting in and out between cars and buses, even veering onto the sidewalk when necessary to avoid gridlock. He had the driver drop him off well away from his apartment and walked the rest of the way.

As he walked, his cell phone rang. He looked at the screen and saw, to his surprise, a picture of Samira Shannon. He almost canceled the call. After everything she had done, why would she contact him? He had once liked and respected her. Then she'd proved herself to be just like all the Americans who came to his country, willing to use their power and wealth to take whatever they wanted.

But Colonel Zhanwei had said she was CIA. If that was true, she would know how to reach people who mattered in the US government. Kit hated the idea of American control of Thailand just as much as Chinese control. But right now, China was the bigger threat. And if China really did have a *living maniraptor* hidden in a cave somewhere that was the source of their domination chemical, then maybe he needed Samira and the United States after all.

He answered the phone. "Samira?"

"Kit! I saw the news. Congratulations!"

For a moment he was stunned. "For what?"

"Science minister? That's incredible. What an honor, and a chance to do some real good."

"Ah, yeah," he said. "Things have changed, I'm afraid. It's been a little crazy here since we last met."

She laughed. "Crazy is right. You'd never believe what I've been doing. I can hardly believe it myself."

"Is it harder to believe than a Cretaceous dinosaur somehow hibernating for sixty-six million years and then coming to life again?" Kit asked.

There was a long pause.

"No," Samira said. "It's exactly that hard to believe."

CHAPTER SIXTEEN

Samira could hardly breathe as Kit described to her what he had learned from the colonel. The Chinese had a maniraptor too! That explained how they seemed to have taken control of Taiwan with such ease. She wondered if it would stop there, or if China would keep expanding their control into neighboring countries.

"What are you going to do now?" she asked.

"I don't know." He sounded stressed and afraid. "They have Mai and Arinya, and I can't do anything about it. I don't have an army. I don't even have any of the chemical. All I can do is lie low and hope they don't find my apartment."

"Isn't there anyone else who can help you?"

"Maybe? There have to be people still loyal to Mai. Thousands cheered her march to the palace, and many more around the country still love her. But I don't know how to contact any of them safely. I could try to reach out to leaders in her organization, but I have no way to tell if they're compromised. Any one of them could be under the control of the Chinese."

"I'm sorry," she said. "That's terrible."

"Is there any way," he began, then tried again. "You have contacts there, right? Is there any way you could help me?"

Samira thought about that. She could hardly believe Everson or any of his superiors would want to help Kit. Though, the more she thought about it, why wouldn't they? Wouldn't they be glad to destabilize China's influence on Thailand? She would be delivering them a real-life foreign intelligence asset, someone high up in the revolutionary government.

"If you had some chemical, what would you do with it?" she asked.

"I would rescue Mai and Arinya," he said immediately. "If I had enough, I would give it to Mai, and she would rule again."

"Let me see what I can do," she said. "To be honest, I'm pretty sure I can't do anything. But let me see."

EVERSON DIDN'T LOOK pleased to see her. She supposed she had earned that.

"I have a gift for you," she said. "For the CIA, I mean."

She told him about her phone call with Kit, the information he had shared about the Chinese maniraptor, and his request for help to rescue the newly-crowned queen. Everson grew increasingly alert, and by the time she finished, he was pacing the room like a jungle cat.

"What are his resources? Can he contact the rest of the resistance?"

"I think he can, but he's afraid to. He doesn't know who's been compromised."

"That's wise." Everson paused. "How do we know *he* hasn't been compromised?"

The thought took her aback. Of course, that was possible.

"Would he tell me about the Chinese maniraptor if he was being controlled by the Chinese?"

"He might. If his story is bogus, it would have us chasing our tails. And if it's true, it could buy him trust."

"It's got to be true. It's not a story you would just make up. No one would believe you."

"Unless they know about ours and want us to think they have one too. Did he tell you where it's being held?"

"A facility in a cave in Yunnan Province," she said. "Probably doesn't narrow it down much, though. Yunnan's a big place."

"But we could look for unusual traffic. If they're distributing the chemical, there would be frequent shipments out of the facility. A cave showing a lot of new traffic on reconnaissance satellite imagery might point us in the right direction."

His pacing was getting on Samira's nerves. "What about Kit, though?" she asked. "Could we get some chemical to him?"

Everson stopped and gave her a look like she was dangerous. "There's no 'we'," he said. "Thanks for the tip, but don't call him again, not unless we manage the call. We have an agent in country who can be his handler; we'll find your friend and make the connection. Where does he live?"

She shrugged. "An apartment. In Bangkok, I would guess."

"Okay, we might need you to call again and get that information, but not until we can do it in a controlled environment, all right?"

"Why can't I be his handler? I already know him; we have a relationship. He'll talk to me."

"Miss Shannon, I'm sure you're very good at what you do, but please. This is what I do. Trust me on this."

She nodded. "All right."

She didn't, though. It had been a mistake to tell Everson. He cared more about Kit's usefulness than his safety. Everson would pass Kit's information on to an intelligence bureaucracy that would see Kit as just a tool they could use. The CIA was going to mismanage the approach somehow and get Kit killed.

Everson had told her not to contact Kit again, but he wasn't in charge of her. She didn't have to listen to him. She had no intention of leaving Kit in the dark until some agent he didn't know tracked him down and expected him to play along with their schemes. The CIA should be helping him, not trying to control him. And if they wouldn't help him, she'd do it herself. But first, she had to talk to Charlie.

THE LAB WAS CROWDED when she got there. Two VIPs, a man and a woman, were standing in the observation deck to watch Charlie feed. Samira didn't know who they were, presumably military bigwigs or congressional staff involved in providing the black budget for this whole operation. She wanted them to leave. It was going to be hard enough to get any time alone with Charlie, and impossible with this kind of attention.

Hunt was there, narrating the show, more gregarious and charming than she'd ever seen him. She played along like a good pet scientist, answering questions about him like a docent at the zoo. The microphones in his cage had been shut off. Apparently, a *speaking* dinosaur was one marvel too many for the bosses to swallow.

Samira thought about switching them on and engaging Charlie in conversation. She wanted to see the shock on their faces, but most of all she wanted them to know: *He's not an animal. He's not a golden goose you can squeeze and out comes a mind-control drug. He's a person.*

She didn't, though. As much as the thought pleased her, she knew she couldn't control what happened next. Instead of a person, they might see him as a threat. A weapon was one thing; an intelligent weapon with its own ideas and agenda might be more than they could accept.

Why wouldn't they just leave? She needed to ask Charlie for help, but she couldn't do that with anyone else around.

Finally, far later than she wanted, the VIPs filed out with Hunt and his staff, leaving her and Paula alone with Charlie.

Paula yawned. "That was two hours of my life I'll never get back. I still haven't finished those budget numbers for Hunt yet."

"Go ahead," Samira said. "I can handle things."

"You're sure?" Paula asked. "We're behind on the cleaning checklist; there's a lot to do here."

"I've got it. Go write up your numbers."

Paula flashed Samira a grateful smile that made her feel a bit guilty. "You're a lifesaver. Seriously, though, call me if you change your mind."

"I've got it," Samira said again. She waved her hand. "Run along, now, I don't need you."

"Fine, if you put it like that," Paula grumbled, but she made her way to the door, leaving Samira alone.

Samira switched the microphones and speakers on immediately. "Hello, Charlie."

"Hello, Samira."

"I have news for you."

"News?" Charlie had no sense of voice inflection, but she was starting to recognize some of the slight scents that he used to characterize his communications. She could *smell* the question mark, and realized he was unfamiliar with the word.

"Yes, news. Um, new information. Something to tell you."

"Tell."

She took a breath. She had already delivered the shattering news that he was the only one left of his species; now she had to tell him she might have been wrong. She had briefly debated withholding the information, but then decided she had to tell him. What if she woke up to discover that intelligent cockroaches ruled the world, and she would never see or speak to another human being again? It was the least she could do to tell him that another of his kind had survived. "There might be—might just possibly be—another one of you. Another one of your species, still alive in the world."

Charlie went rigid, his protofeathers sticking out around his neck, and another flood of scent reached her, though this one she couldn't identify. "Who?" he asked.

The question surprised her, but then she realized he must be making the obvious assumption—that the surviving maniraptor was one he knew. A relatively small number of pits had been built, and Charlie had been instrumental in preparing them and convincing others to use them. His assumption might be right.

"I don't know," she said. "I can't even be certain it's true. I heard from a friend, who heard from another man, who claims to have seen it."

"We go there," Charlie said.

"No. We can't go there. It's on the other side of the Earth." She realized she had never explained to Charlie that he was now thousands of miles away from where his body had been discovered. "If there really is another maniraptor, it's being held by other humans. They won't let us come."

Charlie shifted from foot to foot, growing more agitated. Samira realized it might have been cruel of her to hold out this hope and then snatch it away, when he understood so little of the modern human world. There was very little chance he would ever be reunited with a maniraptor held by the Chinese government. They might never even get confirmation that one existed.

"I have a favor to ask you," she said. "Or at least a question. My friend—the one who told me the news—he's in danger. The people who hold the other maniraptor are looking for him. They are using scent, maybe the scent they took from it, to control and hurt other people, and they want to capture or kill my friend. I want to help him."

It was a long story, and she waited to see if his grasp of English was enough to understand.

"They take scent from other one," he said.

"Yes."

"They use to hurt humans."

"Yes."

Charlie paused. Finally, he said, "You take scent from me."

Samira drew in a sharp breath. He was right, of course. They still put him to sleep on a regular basis and extracted chemicals from his scent glands for military research. She hadn't thought he could know about that, but presumably when he woke, he could feel what had been done. Maybe the process left his glands sore, or less ready to produce scent as usual. She couldn't deny it. She couldn't even protest that the military would use it for good purposes, because she wasn't sure they would.

Her silence lasted too long.

"I'm sorry," she finally said. "That's what the people who run this place want. That's the only reason they keep you alive."

PREY STRUGGLED TO UNDERSTAND. It wasn't just the language, but the human culture and thought process that was hard to grasp. Samira spoke patiently, working around unfamiliar terms, trying to explain to him how her world worked. It was hard for him to wrap his mind around the idea of a world filled with billions of individuals, coordinating their civilization on a scale that dwarfed anything his people had ever done.

She explained about nations—like roosts, only much larger—and how her nation competed for power with another one. She explained how chemicals derived from his body could be used to dominate other humans. He didn't understand, at first. Of course, scent chemicals were used by the strong to dominate the weak. That's how society worked.

But no, of course it wasn't with humans. They dominated each other through words and through technology and the organization and constraints of their society. Chemical domination was a new thing for them, something that subverted existing structures and gave more power to those who controlled it.

"I know you can create chemicals that do many different things," she said. "I saw a memory once where a maniraptor chased away predators by producing a scent that provoked intense fear. Could you create a chemical like that for me?"

He watched her, thinking. The humans already took what they wanted from his body without his permission. He was their prisoner, no matter how well Samira treated him. What would happen if he refused her request? Would they torture him until his body created the chemical they wanted against his will?

"You take it from me?" he asked. "For your leaders to use?"

"My leaders don't know," she said. "I won't force you or take anything against your will. I'm asking for your help so I can help my friend."

WHEN ALEX ARRIVED for the evening shift, Samira headed out.

"Anything eventful?" he asked.

"Not really. VIP tour earlier."

Alex grimaced. "Gotta love those."

She slipped out, taking her bag with her. It looked like a gym bag, but besides a change of her own clothes, it contained a large plastic Ziploc filled with several damp T-shirts. As long as no one opened them or looked too closely, she'd be fine.

She reached her car with nobody stopping her and drove away. She'd almost expected that Everson would have had her under surveillance, and she'd reach the gate to find a dozen military rifles pointing in her direction. No one looked at her twice.

She drove to the nearest post office and got there just before it closed. She pulled a large mailing box from the display and, blocking the view with her body, pulled each Ziploc from her gym bag and carefully closed them all inside. She copied the address of an apartment in Bangkok onto the envelope and approached the front desk. A gray-haired woman in glasses stood behind the counter, stamping packages and tossing them into a bin.

"I'd like to mail this to Thailand, please," Samira said.

The woman rummaged in a drawer and handed her a customs form, which she dutifully filled out. She wrote "six T-shirts" and estimated the value at six dollars.

"Does it contain anything fragile, liquid, perishable, or hazardous?" the woman asked, reciting the words like a mantra.

"Nope," Samira said, though she almost laughed at the question. It was certainly liquid, though most of it was soaked into the T-shirts. It was also arguably one of the most hazardous materials on Earth.

"That'll be $34.65," the clerk said.

"How long will it take to arrive?"

"Six to ten business days."

Samira shook her head. "Is there any way to get it there faster?"

"You can send it expedited. That's three days."

"Let's do that."

The clerk pressed a button. "That'll be $64.27."

Samira handed over the money. As the clerk processed the label, Samira's eyes drifted to the television hanging overhead. BREAKING NEWS, the banner said along the bottom of the screen. The news anchor's cheeks were flushed, and he was almost hyperventilating with the drama of the information he had to convey. The volume was set low, but Samira could make out the words.

"...have just confirmed that the two Americans at Saint Joseph Hospital in Denver have been positively diagnosed. There is no longer any doubt: the Julian virus has made its way to the United States."

Denver. Samira felt something slide sideways in her belly. Saint Joseph was only twenty minutes from her apartment. She gripped the counter for support. The post office clerk heard it, too, and almost dropped Samira's package.

"According to doctors, neither patient had traveled overseas within the last year, leaving the question of how they became infected in the first place as a mystery. Are other residents of Denver walking around with the virus? Or did it arrive via a shipment of food or other material from another country? The CDC is encouraging anyone in Denver who has traveled overseas in the last three weeks and is vomiting or running a high fever to see their doctor. Anyone vomiting blood is especially urged to see a physician as soon as possible."

The hospitals were going to be overrun, Samira thought. She had to get back to the apartment. She had to call Beth. This whole thing had suddenly hit too close to home.

CHAPTER SEVENTEEN

P ak was a traitor, and he knew it. He had been able to convince himself that so much of what had happened in the last year was not his fault. He hadn't meant to kill poor Nikorn. He hadn't meant to become a mule for a drug cartel, or join Princess Sirindhorn's makeshift army. He hadn't chosen any of it; it had simply happened to him. None of it felt like his life.

But he had chosen to betray the princess. He couldn't argue his way around that. He had given that shadowy woman the information she wanted, and she had given him money in return. All the drug labs had been attacked based on his information, and the special chemical stolen. He'd thought the princess's control would collapse after that, but he'd been wrong. She had done the impossible, marched to the palace, and taken over the government with no drugs and no weapons, armed only with the love of the Thai people.

Pak was deeply ashamed of his betrayal. Queen Sirind-horn was a truly good person, one who brought evil men to justice and freed the innocent. She deserved his loyalty. He had thought to take his money and go home, but that would be just another betrayal. She was in trouble. If he could die to protect her, he would do it gladly. His life wasn't worth very much, even to himself, so if it could be useful to her, he would willingly sacrifice it for his queen.

Only she wasn't queen anymore, not really. Those men from China with their smelly flowers and insincere smiles were running things now.

Pak didn't have much education, but he wasn't stupid. He understood that the chemical the Chinese soaked their flowers in was the same chemical the queen herself had used to make the worst of the Red Wa soldiers kill themselves and the others follow her. He even understood that it was the same chemical that had made him hallucinate a giant bird and kill poor Nikorn. Most of all, though, he knew that the queen needed help.

Which was why when he saw Kittipoom Chongsuttana-manee, the former Science Minister and the queen's friend, skulking around the palace grounds, he said nothing. As a guard, it was his duty to report anything suspicious, but he just watched the man instead. He watched him observe the palace each day, and he watched him follow Colonel Zhanwei into the city. He heard the colonel when he returned from that trip disheveled and furious, ordering a warrant for Dr. Chongsut-tanamanee's arrest.

That's when Pak decided it was time to act. He was tired of letting life happen to him. He might never get his old life back, but that didn't mean he couldn't make his new life count for something. If they caught him and he went to prison or died, well, that was no more than he felt like he deserved.

When Dr. Chongsuttanamanee appeared across the street from the palace gate again, Pak was the first to spot him. He left his guard post and crossed to intercept him. When Dr. Chongsuttanamanee saw him coming, he ran, but Pak ran after him. Pak was younger and faster and finally caught him after two blocks.

"Stop!" Pak said. "Wait, I am a friend."

"Let me go. You have no right to hold me."

"I want to help you! I want to help you rescue the queen."

The scientist's face went still. "What makes you think the queen needs rescuing?"

"You know why. She's not in charge anymore. They're making her say whatever they want her to say, and now she's going to marry some Chinese man she never met before. Also, you should stay away from the palace. There's a warrant out for your arrest, after what you did to the colonel. If anybody else besides me spots you, they're going to find a dark hole to throw you in and never let you out again."

"Who are you? And how do you know what I did to the colonel?"

"I'm nobody. Just a guard," Pak said. "I came with you and the queen from Tachileik. Before that I was in Khai Nun. I don't know what you did to Colonel Zhanwei, but I saw you follow him, and he came back furious. If we're going to make a move, we'd better do it before he tracks you down."

Dr. Chongsuttanamanee gave him a calculating gaze. "We?"

Pak shrugged. "The queen needs our help."

The other man was silent for a moment and then shrugged. "Come on."

He led Pak around a corner and into an alley, away from anyone passing by who might overhear. "What's your name?"

"Pak."

"Well, Pak, I need to get into the palace. Is that something you could help me do?"

"Easy."

"Easy? They've got twenty agents with a mind-control chemical, not to mention the whole Royal Army at their beck and call. It might be possible, but it won't be easy."

"I can get you in. That's what's easy. The question is, what will you do then?"

"I'll tell you once we're in," Dr. Chongsuttanamanee said.

Pak crossed his arms. "This isn't going to work if I don't know the plan."

"How do I know you're not going to just turn me in?"

Pak huffed in frustration. For a university professor, the man could be pretty dumb. "If I wanted to, I could have called a dozen soldiers out to chase you down. I wouldn't need to trick you."

"Fine." The man smiled nervously. "It's not exactly a plan. But I have something we can use."

"You have some of the chemical, don't you?" Pak said.

"Not yet. But I should be getting some. It won't be processed in a lab, like what the Chinese are using. It won't control anyone. But it will make them afraid."

Pak thought about that. It might be enough. Or it might not. "I might be able to get some myself. The real kind, like they use."

"From the Chinese? They're not just going to leave it lying around."

"One of them took a mistress from the staff," Pak said. The thought of it made him sick. "He uses the chemical to make her do what he wants. I can convince her to steal it."

"That would be incredibly dangerous for both of you."

Pak got angry. "What's dangerous is her staying in that palace every day. Just because that man likes the look of her, he makes her do anything he wants. He destroyed her life. If she could kill him, I think she would." After all the queen had done to overturn sexual slavery in this country, it was now happening right inside the palace, and no one could do anything about it. Pak wanted to kill them himself.

"Okay," Dr. Chongsuttanamanee said. "Steal it then, if you can, and bring it to me."

"Not so fast," Pak said. "This stuff is the worst invention in history. Worse than all the guns and bombs in the world. It gives men a terrible power, and before I get some of it for you, *doctor*, I want to know what you mean to do with it."

Dr. Chongsuttanamanee placed his hands together and bowed his head in a deep *wai*. "Call me Kit," he said.

"Okay. Kit. What will you do with it?"

"I, too, want to free Queen Sirindhorn, but I want more than that. I want to find the source of this horrible weapon, which Zhanwei tells me is in Yunnan province. And I want to make sure no one can ever control anyone else like this again."

Pak nodded. "Then I'm your man."

IN KIT'S APARTMENT, they shared a meal of Khao Moo Grob bought from a street vendor. Kit wiped the juice from the crunchy pork from his chin with a paper napkin. "So how did you get to be a palace guard?" Kit asked.

Pak told him his story, starting in Khai Nun.

"You!" Kit exclaimed. "You're the one who killed that man for the fossil."

Pak's face went hard. "I did not kill him for the fossil. He was my brother-in-law. You will not believe me, but the fossil made me do it. There was a smell—"

"It terrified you," Kit cut in. "You saw a dinosaur, and it was the most frightening thing you'd ever seen."

"Yes, that's it! It was the dinosaur I shot. But poor Nikorn…"

"I'm sorry. So you ran away and ended up at Tachileik when the princess came?"

"That's it exactly."

A knock on the door made both men sit suddenly upright.

"Friends of yours?" Kit asked.

Pak shook his head. "We could have been followed."

Kit stood and approached the door warily. There was no other way out. Whoever was on the other side knocked again.

"Doctor," the voice said. "I know you're there. I just want to speak with you."

Kit looked through the peephole into the hallway. The man who stood there, features warped by the curved lens, was dressed as an American tourist. And Kit recognized him.

He opened the door. It was the handsome American spy who had visited Mai in the Marriott hotel in Chiang Rai.

The man made a *wai*. "Doctor Chongsuttanamanee," he said. "We meet again."

Stunned, Kit stepped aside and let the man in. "How did you find me?"

The man gave a tight smile. "The US government has its resources."

Kit closed the door. "This is… a friend," Kit said, not wanting to reveal Pak's name.

"Charmed. Perhaps we can talk alone?"

"You can talk in front of my friend," Kit said. "In fact, I trust him more than I trust you. I don't even know your name."

The American gave a tight smile. "You can call me Smith. The reason for my visit, as I expect you can guess, is to renew the offer I made to your queen. My government is prepared to provide you with guns, intelligence, and secure communications as you fight to restore Queen Sirindhorn to power. We ask nothing in return."

"I'm just one person," Kit said, still suspicious. "Two, if you count my friend. What kind of a revolution do you think we can accomplish?"

Smith—or whatever his real name was—smiled. "I know you have been in contact with Samira Shannon. She told us you needed help. That's why I'm here. Earlier you didn't need our help; I understand that. But the situation has changed. We want to see the queen restored as much as you do."

Kit still hesitated. He had asked Samira for this, and he knew he needed the help, but it rankled to have to go to the

Americans and to grant them power and influence over the new government that they were unlikely to give up easily.

Pak had no such reservations. "A real American secret agent from Hollywood!" he said. "Now we'll definitely win." He held out a Styrofoam carton filled with rice and pork. "Want some Khao Moo Grob?"

CHAPTER EIGHTEEN

Julian spread fast, leaving Colorado reeling. Its symptoms were so mild at first that people didn't realize they were sick. Despite the warnings, they unwittingly spread it to families, coworkers, and friends. A week later, those same people would drop in the street, vomiting and convulsing until they died, unable to breathe.

A call from Hunt told them to keep away from the facility. Those who were already at the facility would stay; those at home should shelter in place. Hopefully it wouldn't last long, he said, but Samira could tell he didn't believe it. No one who had lived through the COVID years believed in optimistic predictions of a short quarantine.

The news stories grew worse every day. Samira and Beth watched from their apartment, afraid to go out. The apartment wasn't exactly stocked with provisions for the apocalypse, though, so eventually Samira had to go to the grocery store. The aisles were almost completely empty. Freaked out, she gathered up some of what was left and threw cans in her cart without even looking at the labels.

The death count climbed. Ten deaths were reported in

Denver, then twenty, then fifty. Paris, it turned out, had not contained the virus after all, and it was racing through the 15th arrondissement. The first case in Asia appeared when a Brazilian tourist collapsed in the Hong Kong airport.

They watched the news obsessively. Samira didn't even want to watch, but she couldn't bring herself to turn it off. Nothing else seemed worth doing.

The station ran a special about pets who had caught the virus, and what owners were doing to protect their pets from infection. Wallace sat on Samira's shoulder, watching along with them. She gave him a cracker. "Don't worry," she said. "We'll keep you safe."

Samira worried about Charlie, too. If anyone was safe from the virus, it was him, locked up in his glass cage and only visited by people in hazmat suits. But she missed talking to him, and he would be lonely without her. Did he even know what was happening?

Mom called every day to make sure they were still alive. Gabby called from Stanford, where she and Arun were now living in an apartment together. They could hear him in the background while she talked, shouting questions for her to ask.

"Arun wants to know if you've heard anything from Kit," Gabby said.

"No, but I saw him on TV," Samira said. She hated to lie, but there was no way she could tell Gabby the truth without telling her everything. She wasn't fond of all the security, but neither was she willing to risk being denied access to the lab. "He was named the new queen's science minister or something."

"Crazy," Gabby said. "At least he's probably safe; I haven't heard anything about the virus showing up in Thailand yet. I'm glad you guys are okay."

"Thanks."

"I drove up to Berkeley yesterday," Gabby said. "They finished analyzing our magnetic samples. Chron 29R, just as we expected. That puts our fossils within three hundred thousand years of the K-Pg boundary."

Samira couldn't help it. She let a laugh slip out. Three hundred thousand years was pretty precise for paleontology, but having seen Charlie's dreams… of *course* the fossils were from the end of the Cretaceous. They were, in fact, from its very last year.

"What?" Gabby asked.

"Nothing," Samira said. "Just something struck me as funny." Guilt squirmed in her belly. She hated keeping secrets from the people closest to her about things that mattered to them. "How's your dad doing?" she asked instead.

"Oh, you know," Gabby said. "It's not easy. He wasn't even in the country when Mom died, and that's hard for him."

"For you too, I'm sure."

"We're hanging in there," Gabby said, but there was a hitch in her voice.

"I'm so sorry."

"We'll get through it. A lot of people out there are facing the same thing."

"We miss you."

"Stay safe," Gabby said.

BETH BROUGHT two bowls of soup from the kitchen. "Lentil vegetable," she said. "From a can." Samira blew on it to cool it down and kept watching TV.

Yet another infectious disease specialist was interviewed, this time a Dr. Evelyn Soderberg from the CDC. "What we're looking at is a very ancient survival mechanism," she said. "Some of the earliest life forms on Earth evolved in an anaerobic environment—that's one without oxygen in the air. They stripped oxygen from sulfur oxide compounds and produced hydrogen sulfide gas. The earliest viruses evolved to infect and parasitize those early microbes."

"And you think Julian is one of these ancient viruses?" the interviewer asked.

"Well, it's hard to say, exactly," Dr. Soderberg said. She was young and blond and surprisingly cheerful, given the topic she was discussing. "Like everything else, viruses have evolved quite a bit over the years. But they all operate in essentially the same way: they hijack a cell's machinery and reprogram it to turn it into a factory for more viruses. The largest and most sophisticated viruses can take a cell apart from the inside and completely remake it. The Julian virus is kind of unique, because it remakes cells into the kind those ancient microbes would have had—those that produce hydrogen sulfide gas. Hydrogen sulfide is a broad-spectrum poison that kills like hydrogen cyanide, by preventing cell respiration. For those of us with lungs, it's the respiratory system that goes first."

"But this virus infects things that don't breathe, like fish," the interviewer said.

"That's right!" Soderberg seemed, if anything, to grow more excited and cheerful by the question. "It seems general-ized to go after any eukaryotic cell at all. That's another thing that makes it seem ancient—it's not specialized to particular cell types. It's attacking multicellular organisms on the basis of what we have in common and reconstructing our cells to the kind of ancient cell that it presumably originally evolved to infect."

"But where did it come from? Why is it suddenly affecting us now?"

"Well, we don't really know, but our best guess is that Julian originated in the oceans. Hydrogen sulfide producing bacteria are common there, and Puerto San Julian is, after all, near the sea. It spread so fast that we haven't been able to identify who first contracted the disease, but many of the original victims were fishermen. Scientists have also confirmed that a large portion of the marine life off the Argentina coast is infected with the virus. But how something in the ocean evolved such a universally effective strategy is baffling." Soderberg shrugged and gave the camera a winning smile. "The best we can surmise is that it just got lucky."

The interviewer's generally benign and pleasant face slipped into an expression of disbelief. "Lucky, Dr. Soderberg?"

"Lucky for the virus," Soderberg qualified, dropping the smile and turning red. "It's decidedly not lucky for the rest of us."

The show switched to a shot of a harbor, presumably in Argentina, choked with dead fish bobbing on the waves.

"Marine life has been hit particularly hard by the Julian virus," said the deep tones of the masculine voiceover. "The Argentina fishing industry has collapsed due to contaminated stock, leaving thousands out of work and destroying what for some was a chief source of food. In places that depend on the ocean, famine threatens to kill more than the virus itself."

"This is awful," Samira said. "I had no idea it was this bad."

"That's because you've been living in a hole in the ground, isolated from the rest of the world," Beth said.

"I mean, I knew it was killing people, but I had no idea of the scale, or that it was crossing species boundaries so quickly. What if it gets to the cattle stock in the Midwest? This could create a worldwide hunger crisis even if we do manage to find a cure." Samira thought of Charlie and his efforts to save his species from the coming asteroid. "It could be like the end-Cretaceous extinction," she said. "Or…"

She had just lifted a spoonful of soup to her mouth, but she paused with it held there, her mind racing.

"Samira?" Beth asked. "Are you okay?"

"Gabby's mother was researching the Permian extinction, right?"

"Yeah…"

"And fossils from the end of the Permian period have a lot of hydrogen sulfide."

"They have a high sulfur content, indicating high H_2S levels, yeah."

Samira put the spoon back in her bowl. "What was Gabby's mother doing in Puerto San Julian?"

"She was drilling off the coast. Part of her research into the—"

"—Permian extinction." Samira finished. "And one of the theories about the Permian extinction involves hydrogen sulfide producing bacteria, right?"

"Sure. The idea is that a big volcanic eruption in Siberia depleted the surface oxygen supply in the oceans, which caused the bacteria to thrive on the surface, which increased the hydrogen sulfide content in the oceans, which eventually made its way into the air. The problem with the scenario is just how much gas it would take to choke out all the oxygen breathers in the world. The sky would have to have been green with it."

"What if it wasn't the gas at all? What if the explosion of bacterial life on the surface allowed a bacterial virus to make the leap to marine animals, and from there to animals on land?"

"You're saying the Permian extinction was caused by a virus?" Beth's eyebrows shot up as she made the connection. "By the *Julian* virus?"

Samira stood and started to pace. "Think about it: an ancient virus that came from hydrogen sulfide producing bacteria sweeps through the world, killing every organism in its path, and one of the first people to get it is a Permian extinction expert? Who was drilling into Permian ocean sediment at the time?"

Beth looked at the television, then back at Samira. "She was drilling ocean cores?"

"I think so. Let's call Gabby back."

Gabby confirmed that her mother had been drilling core samples from an abandoned oil rig off the coast, trying to find conclusive evidence for what had caused the Permian extinction.

Samira spoke into the phone. "I think she found it."

CHAPTER NINETEEN

Samira called the CDC and asked to speak with Evelyn Soderberg. As it turned out, quite a lot of people wanted to talk to the CDC, most of them trying to reach specialists who had appeared on television. Samira was informed by an emotionless answer bot that all messages would be reviewed and treated with due seriousness, but that because of extreme call volume, it was not possible for a human to answer the call. The bot then instructed her to visit a hospital immediately if she was showing signs of infection.

The message she left was short and to the point: "I'm a scientist with the University of Colorado in Boulder. I think I know where the Julian virus came from." And she left her phone number. She had no expectation, however, that the message would be reviewed any time soon.

"Who do we know who could get through?" Beth asked.

"Paula," Samira said.

"Paula? She has a contact at the CDC?"

"Not that I'm aware of. But she knows people. She's worth a try, anyway."

Samira called Paula and, after making sure she was still healthy, explained her theory.

"Wow," Paula said. "That's...wow. The worst extinction in history, caused by a highly successful virus."

"I don't know if it's true," Samira said, "and it's not good news for us if it is. If this virus caused the Permian extinction, only a small percentage of the species on Earth survived it, possibly those that had retained an immunity in their genome from when the virus first evolved. Whether or not any such species still exist, it's clear that humanity isn't one of them.

"The people working this at the CDC, USAMRIID, wherever—they've got to know. If Gabby's mother was Patient Zero on this, then they can search the drilling rig, find the original virus before it infected humans, and maybe use that to find a cure. Her team may have collected samples. I left a message with the CDC, but I have no idea when anyone will hear it, and there's no time to lose."

"Let me make some calls," Paula said. "I've got some credibility in high places. I'll make sure the right people know."

AFTER THAT, Samira couldn't sit still. She paced the apartment, twitching with anxiety.

"Do you think we should call the television stations?" she asked. "They would run the story for sure, but if we're wrong, we would just panic people for no reason."

"Give it time," Beth said. "Trust Paula. She won't let it drop, and if she can't get anyone to listen, she'll let you know."

Finally, Samira's phone rang, though the number was unfamiliar. She answered on speakerphone. "Hello?"

An official sounding person said, "Please hold for the Director of the Central Intelligence Agency."

Beth gaped and looked at Samira, who shrugged. A moment later, a man's voice came on the phone.

"Dr. Shannon?" They were both Dr. Shannon, but Samira answered. "Yes?"

"I have heard through channels that you have a theory about the origin of this disease and that it involves the work that Dr. Elena Benitez was doing off the coast of Argentina."

"Yes, sir. She was doing open ocean drilling into the Permian layer. It's just a theory, one which will require disease specialists to verify. If it's true, though, sir—"

"Dr. Shannon, I'm going to have to ask you to keep this information to yourself."

"Sir?"

"I'm going to take care of it. Get it to the right people. But it's not something we want showing up on the evening news, you understand?"

"It's not something we want getting lost in a bureaucratic shuffle, either, sir. This is the fate of the human race we're talking about. At minimum, let me speak to whoever—"

"This isn't a negotiation. As an employee of the CIA, and as an American, I expect you to follow my lead on this. If you recall, you signed some documents to that effect. Revealing classified information comes with serious jail time."

"Classified? I just told *you* this information. I just thought of it myself an hour ago. How can it be classified?"

"It's classified because I just classified it," the director said. "That's how this works."

Samira stared at the phone, confused. Why would the director…

Oh.

"You knew, didn't you?"

The director cleared his throat. "Excuse me?"

"You were funding Elena's research just like you were funding ours. She already had some idea what she might find down there, didn't she? Why else would she be targeting underwater Permian layers? There are plenty of exposed Permian layers on the surface to study. You couldn't pass up the possibility of getting your hands on an ancient, world-destroying virus. You funded her research, and when it got loose, you kept it secret."

The silence stretched. Then the director said, "I'm not a monster. I want this virus stopped the same as you."

"You were keeping it secret to develop as a weapon!"

"Of course we were. Don't be naive, Dr. Shannon. As soon as our enemies think they can attack us without consequence, they will. They have to know they won't succeed. We don't collect weapons to *use* them. They're deterrents to war. That means that any weapon our adversaries could acquire, we have to get first. Until it's fully developed, it has to be a secret, or else they'll know our weaknesses. They'll know what we can't do."

Samira clenched her fists and set her jaw. "It's too late to worry about that. People are dying. This information could help. It's bigger than just the United States. If this is true, the world needs to know about it."

"And I told you I would take care of that. Am I going to have a problem with you?"

She bit her lip. Beth nudged her and nodded at the phone.

"Dr. Shannon?"

"No," Samira said. "No problem."

"Excellent. Then I thank you for bringing this to my attention."

The moment the phone went dead, Samira slammed her fist down on the table. "He's going to bury it," she said, wanting to scream. "This isn't about national security. It's about covering his ass. If he tells anyone at all, it'll be people in the agency who have the wrong qualifications and little experience with the virus. He's just going to hide and hope it blows over."

Samira called Paula back, who picked up on the first ring. "Did someone contact you?" Paula asked.

"Yeah. Was it Everson that you called?"

"Hunt, actually. He's higher up; I thought he could get it up the chain to the top faster."

"He got it up the chain, all right," Samira said. "The director called and told me to keep it quiet. I'm pretty sure he already knew where the virus came from. He's been sitting on it for national security reasons. Or at least so nobody knows that he's partly responsible."

Paula whistled.

"But I *can't* keep it quiet, can I? What if it's someone in China or Russia or Egypt or Turkmenistan that can figure out a cure? I can't just sit on this knowledge and trust the director to do the right thing."

"He probably wants to prevent a panic."

"We already have a panic. People know we can't stop this thing; they say so over and over again on the news. Additional knowledge might give people some hope that we'll figure it out."

"What are you going to do?" Paula asked.

"I don't know," Samira said. "I guess I have to listen to the director." Beth gave her a strange look, but Samira shook her head. "He probably knows more about what's going on than I do."

"Probably for the best," Paula said. "Let me know if you decide to do anything else."

"Okay, will do," Samira said. "Stay safe."

"You too."

When she hung up the phone, Beth raised an eyebrow. "What was that about? You're not going to let it go."

"No. But Paula's in deep with the Agency, and I didn't want her tattling on me. Listen, I bet that neither Paula nor the director actually believe that I'm going to stay quiet any more than you do, so if I want to do something, it needs to be quick."

"What are you going to do?"

She thought about putting what she suspected out on

social media. But she didn't have much of a following, and even if it did get some traction, it would just join the host of conspiracy theories about the virus already bouncing across the internet. No one doing serious work would pay any attention to it. It was too weird, too crazy an idea. But she couldn't just write an academic paper, either. She needed to get the attention of people who might use the information to make a difference, and she needed to do it fast.

Samira looked at the TV, where the news anchors were still talking about the latest body count. "Let's start by calling them."

SAMIRA HAD NEVER VISITED a TV studio before, and had no idea what to expect. An extremely efficient young man took charge of her, speaking constantly as he clipped a visitor's badge to her shirt and whisked her through a series of doorways.

He handed her off to a makeup artist, who pushed her gently into a swivel chair in front of a mirror bordered by large, circular light bulbs. The efficient young man and the makeup artist spoke rapidly about her appearance and how best to fix it as if she weren't sitting right there. She felt like a parcel being passed through an assembly line.

Her makeup was swiftly seen to while a woman behind her did something to her hair. The young man looked at his watch. "Time," he said.

He ushered Samira through another room filled with people and monitors and through another door with a sign that read "Quiet, Filming in Progress."

The next room was vast, like a warehouse, but most of it was dark and painted a matte black, making it hard to see what was in it or how far it stretched. On the other side, taking up maybe a third of the space, was what looked like someone's living room, dazzlingly lit by an array of lights pointed at it from different directions. Several large cameras snaked out of the dark mounted on hinged booms and focused their unblinking eyes on the scene.

On the left, already seated in an easy chair with her legs crossed, was a young woman with a perfect physique and a tailored suit who looked painted into the scene. Samira recognized her as news anchor Kelly Coyle. She looked just as unreal and larger-than-life in person as she did on TV.

"So, how's this going to work?" Samira asked, suddenly feeling like this was a bad idea. It wasn't like she was sure about her conclusion. She just wanted the possibility to be investigated. What if she did incite a panic, like the director warned?

"You'll do fine," the young man said. He unclipped her visitor's badge and held out his arm, directing her to the couch opposite Kelly Coyle.

Samira stared at him. "What, now?"

"Camera rolls in two minutes," he said. "It'll be no problem. You'll do great."

She climbed up to the stage and sat on the couch, feeling profoundly conspicuous in the bright lights. Kelly sat perfectly at ease, reviewing a piece of paper, presumably her opening interview questions. The easy chair and sofa seemed much too brightly colored, as if they were animated set pieces instead of real objects. In her bright green suit and perfect blond hair, Kelly looked the same.

Samira crossed her legs one way, then the other. Should she sit on the edge of the couch? That felt awkward, like she was getting ready to run. But if she sat back, she'd look unengaged. She tried to think how she would sit on a couch normally and couldn't think how to do it.

Someone off stage held up five fingers, then four, then three. Kelly handed her review sheet to an aide and looked straight into the camera, unhurried, her position on the chair somehow seeming both poised and utterly relaxed at the same time. Samira wished desperately for a drink of water.

While Kelly delivered her opening remarks, Samira tried to review what she intended to say, but her mind had gone blank. All she could think about was her own physical anxiety: Where should she look? Should she smile? Where should she put her hands?

Finally, Kelly directed her larger-than-life smile at Samira and said, "In the studio today we have famed paleontologist Samira Shannon, who found an entire nesting site full of dinosaur eggs in Thailand five years ago. Dr. Shannon, what have you been up to since then?"

"A lot more digging," Samira said, with a nervous smile that felt fake. That first find had earned her a lot of articles and calls from journalists, and one interview on NPR, but never television before now. She was surprised by how different it was. "I've led several more expeditions to the Khorat Plateau in Thailand, which is one of the world's most exciting new fossil locations."

"You didn't come here to tell us about one of your fossil finds, though," Kelly said. "You came because you believe you know the source of the Julian virus."

Samira took a deep breath. "That's right. I want to emphasize that this is a theory, one that I myself am in no position to verify one way or another."

"Because you're stuck in Denver like the rest of us," Kelly said.

"Yes. But as a scientist studying the deep past, it looks like a real possibility to me. About 250 million years ago, something nearly killed all life on Earth. Almost everything living was affected, on land and in the oceans. Most of them died. It's called the Permian Extinction, or just the Great Dying. We don't know what caused that. But now we're facing this virus with similar characteristics: it crosses species boundaries, killing everything from humans to hummingbirds. So maybe it's the same."

"Viruses can't usually affect so many species like this, can they?"

"No, that's right. Most viruses have evolved in tandem with their hosts for millions of years, so they're tailored to infect only them. Some can jump species boundaries, but never so many species at once. But if this is a truly ancient virus, then it makes more sense. It's a virus that's common to all our ancestors, only it's been so long, we've lost any defenses our ancestors might once have had against it."

"So you think the Julian virus spreading around the world now is the same virus that killed all those animals back before the dinosaurs?" Kelly asked. "Do you have any proof?"

"Not proof, no. More like circumstantial evidence. One of the first people infected was a scientist named Dr. Elena Benitez. She and her team had been drilling into the layer of sedimentary rock formed during the Permian era. We can't tell exactly what she found, though, because she and her team are all dead."

"A killer virus, raised from the deep?"

Samira nodded. "One that very nearly eradicated all life on the planet 250 million years ago."

"Are you telling us there's no hope? That we're all going to die?"

"No! I don't even know if I'm right about this. I'm trying to get the word out to medical researchers around the world that this is a serious possibility. It would explain how it jumps from species to species, and why it's so much more deadly than COVID. If it can be verified that the disease started on board Dr. Benitez's ship, then that brings us one step closer to finding a cure."

"And what will happen if we don't find a cure?"

Samira was taken aback. She wasn't expecting the question. The answer seemed kind of obvious, but she didn't want to say so on television. "Disaster response isn't my area of expertise," she said. "There are people whose job it is to make decisions about evacuation, quarantine, containment, that sort of thing."

"But you're saying the death count could be extremely high. In the millions? Billions?"

"I don't know. It could be very high."

"Is our survival as a species at risk?"

"We should take that possibility seriously," Samira said. "I don't have the expertise, but I'm talking to those who do: Please investigate this. Look into Dr. Benitez and her team. Examine the drilling rig they were on. Test ancient animals for immunity. We have to act fast. This might be the scariest thing we've ever faced as a species."

Kelly's professional face showed a carefully-crafted expression of shock. "Should we be getting out of Denver?" she asked.

"No. Again, I'm not a specialist, but I'm sure the experts would tell you to stay inside and stay calm. The more people move around, the faster the disease will spread."

"Thank you, Dr. Shannon." She faced the camera. "You heard it here first: the scariest disease we've ever faced. Stay safe, everyone. This is Kelly Coyle."

The cameras went dark, and Kelly grinned at her. "That was great. Thank you so much. We'll be worldwide news by ten o'clock."

Samira left the studio in a daze, wondering if she should have listened to the CIA Director after all.

CHAPTER TWENTY

The morning after Samira's appearance on television, the military arrived in Denver in force. Humvees and armored patrol vehicles lined up on the highways and barricaded intersections. The perimeter stretched from Fort Collins in the north to Castle Rock in the south. Routes 25, 70, 270, and 76 were closed to all non-military traffic.

In a television address, the state governor announced that, with the help of the Army and the federal government, the municipalities of Denver, Aurora, and Boulder were being placed under forced quarantine. All flights in and out were canceled. Non-essential personnel were instructed to stay in their homes.

Normally-crowded streets emptied of traffic, while on television, endless images of vehicles with machine guns and grenade launchers paraded past with suburban developments in the background. Every shot seemed to include a McDonalds or a baseball diamond or an elementary school with US flag flying, as if to emphasize: *This is happening in America.*

Samira sat glued to the screen, stricken.

"You did the right thing," Beth said. "This was going to

happen anyway. If you sped up the timeline, that might even be for the best."

"I just hope someone can find a cure."

"Don't we all."

Army personnel stopped food delivery trucks at the perimeter and drove them to distribution centers. Hospitals filled with the infected. Clinics appeared all over the quarantined area, giving people a place other than the hospitals to be tested. Many doctors from outside the quarantine willingly entered it to help staff these, even though they would not be allowed to leave again.

Despite their best efforts, it was an impossible perimeter to maintain. Even a place like Denver, with the mountains as a natural barrier and a large nearby military presence, had too many roads in and out to completely corral a frightened populace. People determined to get out would find a way.

A few days later, a case was diagnosed in Grand Junction, near the Utah border. Someone had gotten out through the mountains and had brought the virus with them.

"How can they even stop it?" Beth asked. "This thing can infect birds. What are they going to do, cordon off the sky?"

More cases turned up in North Platte and Omaha, and then, terrifyingly, in New York City.

PAULA CALLED. It took Samira a moment to realize she was crying.

"You couldn't wait, could you? You couldn't listen!"

"Paula, are you okay? Are you sick?"

"Sick? No. Not yet. But they're shutting us down."

"What do you mean?"

"They're discontinuing the program. Permanently."

Samira rocked back from the phone. *Permanently?* "But...what about Charlie?"

"They're going into 'full scale development' mode. It means they're going to strap him down and engineer situations to make him produce the chemical in large quantities. They're going to hurt him, in other words. No more talking, no more science. Just torture and extraction."

"There must be some mistake."

"No mistake. There were always some who thought a science team was a waste of time. Everson, for one. They've been lobbying the director to scrap it for months. After your little stunt on national news, he's ready to listen. They convinced him we're a security risk and a needless hindrance, and he's shutting us down."

"They're going to end up killing him, and then they'll have nothing. No scientific understanding, and no Charlie, either."

"That line of reasoning worked for a while, but not anymore. Hunt used to listen to me, or at least humor me. He let me continue that side of the project, despite the expense, because I convinced him it might give us more unique knowledge. But they don't care about the science. They don't care about what things were really like in the Cretaceous, or about preserving the last of a species. He's just a weapon to them."

"But he can *talk*. He's a person. They can't just torture him."

"Who's going to stop them?" Paula took a breath and lowered her voice. "To tell the truth, they never planned to let us go very much longer anyway. I was buying a week at a time, begging the money out of Hunt to keep it all going."

"You never told me."

"Hunt is mostly on my side, I think, but as far as his superiors are concerned, the science team is nothing but an impediment and an expensive security risk. The CIA isn't set up for operations that include acquiring and transporting live deer on a regular basis in secret. They've wanted us gone for a while."

Samira paced the room, clutching the phone in a death grip. "We've got to do something."

"There's nothing to be done. Honestly, I think you've done quite enough."

"Don't put this on me! I was trying to save lives. Possibly billions of them."

Paula sighed. "I know. But what do you think I can do? Sneak him out in my pocket? Even if I could, where would he go? The Denver Zoo?"

"Are you at the facility right now?"

"For the moment. I'm packing up my things."

"Don't leave yet. I'm coming."

"What are you going to do?"

"I don't know. At the very least, I'm going to say goodbye."

"THIS ISN'T A GOOD IDEA," Beth said. "You should stay here. You can't do anything there, and if you go, they might just decide to arrest you."

"I have to go. I can't let this happen to Charlie without at least talking to him one last time."

"Tell me you'll behave. That you won't try to take on the military single-handed and fight your way out."

"I'm just going to say goodbye."

Beth smiled grimly. "Okay, then. Good luck. Come back safe."

Samira drove toward the mountains, hoping she wouldn't be stopped by the Army maintaining the quarantine. Technically, the facility was outside the quarantine zone, but she doubted the way there was blocked. There was barely a road.

She dug her fingernails into the steering wheel and tried to avoid the temptation to floor the accelerator. They were going to end up killing Charlie. They weren't thinking of him as a person at all, or even as something unique to be protected. Maybe the recent successes at bringing back species had jaded them to the idea of extinction. Now that we had its DNA, we could just make another one, right? No big deal.

She replayed the events of the last few days in her head and tried to think what else she could have done, and whether it would have turned out better. She could have trusted the director, of course, and kept quiet, but that meant risking the fate of the human race on a bureaucrat's willingness to share information. A bureaucrat who was willing to torture an intelligent creature to get what he wanted. She could have kept calling disease centers directly until she got through, but that would have taken more time, and with possibly limited effect. No, she had to believe she'd done the right thing. Now everyone knew.

Her phone rang, startling her nearly out of her skin. She fumbled it out of her pocket and held it up to her ear with one hand while driving with the other.

"Hello?"

"Dr. Shannon?"

"Yes."

"This is Dr. Soderberg at the CDC. You left a message for me."

"Hi! Yes, thanks for calling back."

"I'm sorry, your message wasn't passed on to me until after I'd seen you on TV."

"That's why I did it. The TV show, I mean. I wasn't sure I could get through to anyone otherwise. Do you think I'm right about the virus?"

"There's a chance of it," Soderberg said. "It fits the facts I know, at any rate. I was calling to see if you knew anything more than you were able to say on TV."

Samira thought of everything she had learned about the existence of an intelligent culture long before humanity. None of that seemed relevant, though. "I don't know anything," she said. "I'm just connecting the dots."

"I was afraid of that," Soderberg said. "Well, you have my personal number now, if you connect any more of them."

"Is anyone looking into Dr. Benitez's expedition?"

"We've made contact with some people down there, and it seems likely that the crew of her rig were the first to contract the disease, as you guessed. I'm not sure how it helps us, though. If it's really been hiding out for 250 million years, that explains why it's so different than anything we've encountered before. But it doesn't get us any closer to a cure. When the source is an animal, we can capture it and maybe derive an antiviral, but that doesn't work when it comes from a hole in the ground."

"What if you had an animal that was immune? Would that help?"

"It might," Soderberg said. She sounded interested. "It depends what you mean by immune. We have animals and humans who have gotten sick and then recovered, of course. The mortality rate is frighteningly high, but it's not 100%."

"I was thinking more on the species level," Samira said. "Horseshoe crabs, for instance, were around during the Permian, so somehow they survived this virus when everything around them died. Of course, *everything* alive today is descended from something that survived the Permian, but most species have changed radically since then. Horseshoe crabs haven't changed—genetically, they're still more-or-less the same as they were 250 million years ago. If the Julian virus is really what caused the Great Dying, then horseshoe crabs should be immune."

"Horseshoe crabs."

"Well, lampreys and a few kinds of jellyfish are that old, too. Maybe a shark or two. Horseshoe crabs are probably the easiest to get."

"I can't say our lab has ever tried to obtain horseshoe crabs, but I'll see what we can do. Thank you, Dr. Shannon."

"I hope you figure this out."

Soderberg gave a dry laugh with no humor in it. "So do I."

SAMIRA DROVE through the black wilderness, her headlights illuminating only a small patch of sandy path. She hoped she'd be able to find the facility in the dark. It wasn't like there were any signs or bright lights to tell her where it was. Just her luck, she'd end up lost in the mountains somewhere and never be heard of again.

Her phone rang again, startling her a second time. "Hello?"

It was Paula. "Don't bother coming," she said. "They're revoking your access."

"What? Already?"

"Hunt said the director was very specific on that point. You can't get in."

A male voice in the background said, "Is that Dr. Shannon? Give me the phone."

Samira hoped it was Alex, but instead, the unmistakable voice of Adam Hunt came on the line. "Listen, Dr. Shannon, you've been denied access here. Starting at midnight tonight, the change will go into effect, and the doors will no longer open for your badge. Do you hear me?"

Midnight tonight? "Are you saying…"

"I'm not saying anything, Dr. Shannon, except to stay away from this facility. Tomorrow morning, your patient will be removed, and it will be too late."

"So tonight…"

"No one will be here tonight. The facility is shutting down."

"I understand, sir."

"Goodbye, Dr. Shannon."

She thought about it, her heart racing. If he was saying what she thought he was saying, then she had until midnight.

Mind made up, she turned the wheel hard, kicking up sand in a sudden U-turn. She didn't want this visit just to be a last sad farewell. She was going to get Charlie out of there. And if her access cut off at midnight, that didn't leave her much time.

She flicked her phone on and pushed one of the quick dial options. It rang and rang until finally her dad answered. "Samira? Are you okay?"

"I'm fine, but I need a favor. It's important. Do you still have that big truck you use for Goodwill deliveries?"

"Sure, what do you need it for?"

Samira grimaced, wondering how she could explain. "You're not going to like it."

CHAPTER TWENTY-ONE

Kit was on the verge of doing something stupid. He'd been holed up in his apartment for days, avoiding search parties. He had little to do but watch TV and wait until Samira's package arrived. Even the TV had little appeal, since he kept seeing his own face plastered on it—not the recent photos of him in his military regalia, but an awful university professor shot that made him look like a terrorist. Zhanwei didn't forgive easily, and he'd turned Kit into public menace number one.

The CIA had pressed him hard, as Samira had warned him they would. The idea of working with a foreign intelligence service to attack his own country's government made him profoundly uneasy, but what choice did he have? Thailand was not free. There was no Thai government now, not really. And he couldn't do much about that without help.

Anything at all could be happening to Mai and Arinya, and Kit wore a rut into the cheap carpet in his apartment, pacing back and forth in frustration and fear. Each day that passed, he was tempted to make the attempt without Samira's package, but he knew their chances would be desperately small. If all he did was get himself killed, he wouldn't be any good to anyone.

A lot of the TV coverage was about the Julian virus, which had now reached twenty-seven countries. All the old COVID battle lines about quarantines and masking and keeping kids out of school had collapsed under the sheer lethality of Julian. Most people who contracted COVID-19 had survived with only mild effects, allowing disagreements about how serious to take it to grow into political feuds. Julian, on the other hand, killed almost everyone it touched, the young as easily as the old. If the doomsayers could be believed, it might even threaten the extinction of humanity altogether. Compared to this lion at the gates, COVID-19 had been a kitten.

The scene on the television switched to a news studio, and suddenly, there was Samira Shannon. He watched, transfixed, as she presented a theory for the origin of the virus, as forceful and articulate as he remembered her. The Permian extinction. Was it possible? The thought made Kit shiver despite the warmth of his apartment.

He remembered when the magnitude of that extinction event had first struck him, as an undergraduate, while examining a collection of trilobite fossils. Trilobites were about as rare as acorns—in the right places, you could gather them by the bucketful. Thousands of different species of trilobite had populated every marine ecosystem on the planet from the tropics to the Arctic. They were as varied and ubiquitous as the modern beetle, some as big as puppies and some barely large enough to see. Then suddenly, they were gone. From billions covering the globe to complete extinction in the blink of an eye. Their commonness in the fossil record prior to 252 million years ago, and their complete absence afterwards, had made a profound impression on him. No matter how widespread a type of animal became, it could still go extinct.

A knock on the door made him jump. "Professor!" came Pak's voice through the door.

Kit opened it. "Shh," he said. Let's not announce our presence to the whole apartment building, okay?"

"Okay, okay. But look!" Pak held up a cardboard box plastered with stamps and a plastic envelope with customs forms. "It came!"

Kit smiled as he opened the box and pulled out the chemical-soaked T-shirts, each in its own doubled Ziploc bag. Samira had come through for him.

This chemical wasn't the same as the others. The chemical they had all used so far communicated dominance, establishing position in the maniraptor social hierarchy. It had been derived from the signature tag that accompanied all of the stored memories from the pit. But maniraptors communicated all sorts of things with all sorts of chemicals, including the presence of danger, ownership of land or material, or a desire to mate. Samira knew that, and she had convinced her maniraptor to produce something different for Kit.

He held it up for Pak to see.

Pak eyed it skeptically. "How do you know if it works?"

Kit shrugged. "Try it, I guess."

KIT WASN'T sure how far he could trust Pak, but at this point, he didn't have any choice. The man didn't have much education, but he certainly knew more about smuggling than Kit did. He knew how to find the right people to bribe, and how to spot the routes into the palace that no one else would think about. The Chinese might be powerful, but they couldn't be everywhere at once. They certainly couldn't personally check all of the shipments of food and supplies brought into the building.

The palace residence where they held Mai and Arinya had been built in 1890 with no thought for air conditioning, but a ventilation system had been introduced in the 1950s which had later been used to provide central air. Pak led Kit to the cellar where the blowers were.

"Let's hope this works," Kit said. He was actually afraid it would work too well. He had tried it out himself the night before, with Pak watching over him, and the results had been astonishing. He'd taken only the tiniest sniff, but the effect in his mind and body was immediate: *Run! Run! Run!*

There was no terror in it; he didn't scream or panic. He just felt an overwhelming sense that danger was nearby, coming for him, and he needed to get out of there fast. It didn't matter that he knew there was no actual danger; the smell affected him on a core, animal level and insisted that he take flight or die. If Pak hadn't tackled him, he would have run out of the room and the building entirely, heedless of the attention he drew.

Kit placed the chemical in the ventilation system and turned up the blower. The scent should be subtler this way than the direct sniff he had taken. He didn't want the urge to evacuate the building to be so strong that people threw themselves out second- or third-story windows.

"Now we wait, I guess," Kit said.

Kit paced, listening to the sounds above, waiting for a response.

It didn't take long. The sound of stampeding feet above them told Kit the chemical was working its magic. He hoped no one trampled anyone else in their haste to leave.

"Let's go," Kit said. Armed with nose plugs, they ran up the stairs into a scene of chaos. Palace officials and servants and guards streamed out of the doors, shouting and pushing each other to get through.

"Come on, this way," Pak said.

PAK'S HEART WAS HAMMERING. The palace was a maze of rooms and passageways, but he knew exactly where to go. He had spent much of his time as a guard learning how the palace was laid out and where the queen was kept. But he had no explanation if he was challenged. Not for why he was heading into that section of the residence, and especially not for why he was escorting a wanted traitor there.

Fortunately, no officials stopped them. The people they did see paid no attention to them as they rushed past, focused instead on leaving the building as quickly as possible.

Pak hurried on. "The queen is this way."

"Wait, we have to get their supply of the chemical first," Kit said. "Otherwise, there'll be no stopping them."

Pak narrowed his eyes, mistrustful. "I don't care about that. I'm here for the queen."

"I am, too. But getting the chemical will help us rescue her."

"Or it'll get us killed."

"Okay," Kit said, "We split up. Just tell me where they keep it."

"I don't know," Pak lied. "We'll have to rescue the queen and ask her."

On the third floor, they reached the door for the wing of sumptuous rooms that was her prison. It stood open. A quick look inside showed a wide hallway with elaborate mirrors and portraits and several more doors. At the other end stood two Chinese men that Pak assumed from the flowers in their lapels wore the domination chemical. He couldn't see their nose-plugs from here, but judging by the fact that they weren't running, they must have them, too. Both were armed.

Out of sight around the doorway, Pak took a deep breath. This is where it got real. He was not a violent man, despite his earlier life as a smuggler. He had shot his brother-in-law out of terror and self-preservation, not anger, and although he knew how to use a gun, he had never intentionally used one on another person. He lifted his pistol from its holster, and from a hook on his belt, he pulled a grenade.

"Whoa," Kit said. "Where did that come from?"

"This is what it's going to take," Pak said. "Are you with me?"

Kit pulled out the pistol Pak had stolen for him and raised it awkwardly. The man was a professor and looked the part. He held the gun like it was an animal that might bite him.

"Just don't shoot me," Pak said. "You ready?"

Kit nodded, his face ashen.

Pak slipped a well-worn photo of Kwanjai out of his breast pocket and kissed it. *This is for you*, he thought. *So you grow up living in a better world.*

He pulled the pin from the grenade and tossed it down the hall. He heard it rattling as it bounced and rolled, and the shouts of the men who saw it coming. He waited for the explosion, then rounded the corner, pistol raised.

THE GRENADE WAS LOUDER than anything Kit had ever heard. He ran after Pak, his ears ringing and the world gone false color, like he was watching this happen to someone else on a bad television. Pak fired down the hallway, but Kit just ran, too terrified to lift the gun, much less aim it at a human being.

As it turned out, shooting was unnecessary, since the grenade had already done its grisly work. Kit tried not to look at the bodies. These men had kidnapped Mai and forced her to say and do what they wanted. They deserved what they got. But that didn't mean Kit had to like it.

"You ready?" Pak asked. He burst through the door, gun drawn, and this time Kit managed to lift his gun and follow him. The room held only Mai, against the far wall, her arms covering her head, and Arinya, who shielded the queen with her own body.

"We're friends," Kit said. "Mai, Arinya, it's me. We're getting you out of here. Here, put these in—" he handed them each a pair of noseplugs.

After fitting hers into her nose, Mai jumped to her feet, her eyes on fire. "It's about time." She wore American jeans and a tank top, a marked contrast to the elaborately embroidered gowns and jewelry she'd worn every time they brought her out for show. "Give me that," she said, and snatched the gun out of Kit's hand.

"We've got to get their supply of the chemical," Kit said.

"You didn't get that already?" Arinya asked. "How did you get in here then?"

"No time to explain."

Mai was already halfway out the door, gun raised. "Let's go."

THE HALLS of the palace were eerily deserted. Kit, Pak, Mai, and Arinya headed for the royal vault, where many of the royal family's jewels and other treasures were kept. The Chinese hadn't changed the biometric security yet; they had Mai under their control, so they just forced her to open it when they needed to. She placed her hand on the panel, and the light by the door switched to green.

She hauled the heavy door open, gun ready, but there was no one inside. Kit followed her and saw beautifully lit and arranged jewelry, exquisite Buddhist statuary, and on one table, an open metal suitcase containing vials of the domination chemical. Arinya opened one and doused each of them, then Kit closed and locked the suitcase and lifted it. It was heavier than he expected, but not so heavy he couldn't manage it.

Outside, crowds of people from the palace had gathered in the gardens, looking up at the buildings. In the fresh air, the fear had probably dissipated, but they stood frozen, unwilling to reenter until someone told them the danger had passed.

Mai walked out the front doors, no less regal for her casual attire. She strode confidently through the crowd, which had grown larger from tourists and other onlookers gathering to see what was happening. As her scent spread, they quieted.

"Be calm," Mai said. "Everything is under control now. Which of you has access to the armory?"

An older man in a guard's uniform raised his hand.

"Good. Take ten men with you and bring weapons for everyone here. We have been invaded by a foreign power. It's time to take our country back."

The people gave up a cheer as the guard ran off at a trot to do as Mai instructed. Soon he and his compatriots were back with armfuls of weapons that they distributed throughout the crowd.

"I am Somdet Phra Rajini Srinagarindra Chakri Sirind-horn," she declared in a carrying voice. Kit and Pak stood at either side. "I am *not* engaged to marry Zhang Hai, nor have I forged an alliance with China, our oppressor to the North. I was kidnapped and forced to say these things against my will. But never again! We will start from this place and we will make Thailand ours again."

Another cheer went up from the crowd. They held machine guns and automatic rifles over their heads and shook them and screamed Mai's name.

"We will root the Chinese out from wherever we find them. They will not violate our sovereignty again!"

Kit winced at that, thinking of all of the Thai citizens of Chinese descent that Mai had just put in danger. Would these people, or the many others she recruited to follow them, make a distinction between ethnic Chinese and actual Chinese spies? How many innocent people would die?

Before he could voice his concern, though, a flare went off in the square beyond, drawing all eyes. Ranks of soldiers approached at a jog, wearing PRC military uniforms. They wore gas masks, and they were clearly professionals. More soldiers came in from the right and left, surrounding them. Kit had been expecting mostly Thais dominated by a handful of Chinese. But once the Chinese were in control, they must have brought in their military. They controlled the queen, after all. Who would have stopped them?

Kit despaired. He and Pak had delayed too long. A few days earlier, and maybe they could have established control, but now. Now it was too late.

"Ready your arms!" Mai screamed. "Prepare to fire!"

The ragged crowd of palace servants, cooks, tailors, secretaries, and chamberlains, unable to resist Mai's commands, lifted weapons to their shoulders and aimed them at the newly-arrived troops. The Chinese army lifted rifles as one, like a machine.

"Don't do it," Kit said. "We can't win."

Mai's eyes were wild. "I'm not going back into that room. I won't let them control me like that, not ever again."

"The army will kill them all and still capture us. Don't make them die for nothing."

Mai stared at the oncoming army, her face twisted in anguish and indecision.

"Your majesty!" Kit shouted.

She deflated. Kit saw the moment that she made the right choice, to surrender instead of driving untrained civilians to attack professional troops. At least, he thought he did. He would never know for sure.

Before she could order them to drop their weapons, the chatter of automatic weapons fire cut through the air. Kit threw himself to the ground, thinking the Chinese had opened fire, but no: the Chinese were falling. Their troops turned around, shooting *behind* them, flanked by an unknown force.

"*Fire!*" Mai yelled.

The makeshift army let loose with their weapons. The Chinese soldiers ran for cover, suddenly outmaneuvered. Kit stayed on the ground, his arms over his head. Whatever brave thoughts he might have had about sacrificing himself for the queen were blasted out of his mind by the noise and smoke and screams and the sheer terror of hot slugs of metal piercing air and flesh around him.

Thai soldiers flooded into the square along with ordinary civilians with guns of their own. They forced the Chinese back, shouting, "For the queen!" Kit lifted his head slightly to see. The American agent had come through for them after all. He had contacted what was left of Mai's resistance, supplied them with weapons, and told them their queen needed them. Neither the ground assault nor their rescue would likely have succeeded on their own, but together, it was enough.

Kit pulled himself up from the ground. Mai had never left her feet. Smudged with dirt and waving her rifle like an American movie heroine, she shouted and whooped as the Chinese fled. "Take prisoners!" she yelled. "We want the world to see what's happened here."

Kit took a deep breath and let it out again, trying to still his pounding heart. They had done it. Mai was queen again.

CHAPTER TWENTY-TWO

Samira met her father in the empty dirt parking lot of the Larkspur Pizzeria and Cafe, probably the only restaurant for twenty miles in any direction. "We serve fresh Minnesota Walleye," the sign read. "Live music every Wednesday and Friday night."

Since the secret facility was outside the quarantine zone, she'd been able to make her way south along mountain roads and come out here, south of the quarantine, avoiding the blocked intersections. When she pulled in to the lot, bumping over the uneven dirt surface, her father was already waiting for her. She waved, parked, and got out. Hopefully her car would still be here when she got back. If she ever did.

She climbed into his truck, a boxy white Isuzu with a rear door that lifted on tracks. Dad wore a red flannel and a Rockies ball cap and looked every inch a trucker. With all the food and supplies being shipped to Denver these days, nobody would look at him twice.

"Thanks for doing this, Dad," she said, and she meant it. Not many people would jump in a truck and drive toward a quarantine zone with zero explanation, but she'd known he'd do it. She was just surprised Mom wasn't along for the ride.

Samira directed him toward the mountains and onto Route 105 so they could circle around Denver again and avoid the roadblocks. He pulled the Isuzu into gear and took to the road without question.

"So why didn't Mom come?" Samira asked once they were on their way.

"Ah, she was tied up with some stuff and feeling pretty tired. Besides, the cab only has two real seats."

That surprised Samira. As long as she'd known her, Mom would move heaven and earth for a chance to see one of her daughters. But he was right about the truck—there was a kind of bench behind the seats where someone could sit sideways with their legs pulled up, but only the two seatbelts. That was probably why.

"Is she okay?"

"What? Yeah. She'll be fine. Just tired is all. She's been working a lot of hours."

"Long hours? Why?"

He looked surprised. "All the non-profits are working over-time to send relief supplies to Denver. Your Mom's right in the thick of it, organizing and making calls and coordinating. I've been up and back with this truck a dozen times, hauling food and medical supplies."

Of course she was. "She's a good person," Samira said.

"Always."

Which got her thinking about her parents again, and why they drove her so crazy, despite their obvious love for her. She wanted to feel free to pursue her own passions, but somehow their charitable work made her love of science seem trite. How could you argue with helping the needy? How could she say her work was valuable in the face of that? But she was good at science, and it was what she loved. She didn't think it was a wrong thing to pursue. So why did being with her parents always make her feel guilty? Was it their fault, or was she just doing it to herself?

Her mind was so deep in the same mental rut that she almost forgot to tell her dad where to go.

"Turn here!" she said.

"What, to the left? Rainbow Creek Road?"

"That's it."

He made the turn and drove on. They wound through the country toward the mountains, with nothing but dirt and scrub brush on either side. The roads got smaller and dustier and then turned suddenly steep as they reached the foothills.

"I saw you on TV," he said after a while.

"Yeah. Not everybody was happy about that."

"I'm sure you did what you thought was best."

She paused and then said, "Do you believe me? About the virus?" Maybe it wasn't fair to put him on the spot, but she wanted to know. She had never doubted his love for her, but his disappointment with her life choices hung in the air of every conversation. At least they did for her.

"I know a bit about viruses," he said, which was true. As a doctor in the developing world, he had seen and treated all manner of diseases. "They're hardy little critters. Norovirus can survive for weeks on a dry surface. Just when you think you've got an outbreak licked, people start coming down with it again. So yes, given some mud and a bacterial culture, I'm sure a virus could stay viable for years, even deep underground."

"Not just years, Dad. *Millions* of years. Hundreds of millions."

He shrugged. "Don't know that it makes much difference. The important thing is treating it. Finding a cure or a vaccine and keeping the sick away from the healthy until we do."

She huffed in frustration. "How can you do that?" She knew she should just let it go, especially when he was doing her a favor, but she had too much stress and emotion built up to just brush it under the rug.

"Do what?"

"Not care enough about truth to examine the science. The Earth is *old*, Dad. Billions of years old. Everything points to it. The stars, the rocks, the mountains, the oceans, the plants and animals: everything. You're a smart guy. If you spent half a day looking at the evidence, you'd see it."

He shook his head and gave her that calm, kindly smile that always infuriated her. "Sami, I don't need to."

"What, because the Bible says it was created in six days? That doesn't make all the evidence go away. Things are either true or they're not. You taught me that. So it can't be both. Either the world was created all at once a few thousand years ago, or it wasn't."

"I don't need to know anything about rocks or fossils to know what's true."

"But you won't even—"

"Listen to me. For the last fifty years, the one constant in my life is that God has been there for me, no matter what. Your mother and I have had good times and bad ones, we've lived in comfort and we've feared for our lives, but time and again, I've seen God answer prayer. Jesus Christ is alive and at work, and no amount of carbon dating and DNA analysis is going to convince me otherwise.

"So yeah, there might be something to all this fossil evidence. Beth certainly thinks so. Maybe God created it with all those fossils there, or maybe there's another explanation. But it doesn't matter. I don't feel the need to study it, because it's not a threat to what I believe. Trying to figure out which way it works doesn't interest me all that much. It's irrelevant to the fact that Jesus Christ is king of the universe. And my heart."

To Samira's horror, his cheeks were wet with tears. And here she was, once again feeling like the lousy daughter for pushing him on it. "Oh, Dad."

He wiped at his face with the back of a hand. "I just wish you understood that for yourself."

She tried to apologize, but he waved her off and took a deep breath. "Now. Do you want to tell me where we're going?"

SHE TOLD HIM EVERYTHING. There was no point holding back. If he wasn't going to go through with it, she might as well know now. But as she expected, he didn't balk; he just listened to her account and asked a few careful questions.

"So this creature that talks to you," he said. "Is it dangerous?"

She thought about it. "I'd have to say yes. If he wanted to kill me, he could do it easily. But humans can be dangerous, too. It doesn't mean he'll hurt anyone. And it doesn't mean he should be mistreated."

They cut through a ranch and into Roxborough State Park, where giant red rocks jutted up out of the countryside at sharp angles. The rocks were all that remained of the Ancestral Rockies, an older version of the Rocky Mountains that had spanned roughly the same region three hundred million years earlier. Iron oxide and pink feldspar gave them a reddish hue that contrasted stunningly with the green aspens and blue sky. The setting sun glared in and out from between them as they navigated the twisting road.

Her phone rang, and she checked the screen. "Hi, Paula."

"Hunt's gone home, and most of the other staff as well. Alex and I are still here. Where are you?"

"We'll be there soon. Thirty minutes."

They hugged the mountains and weaved their way north. Samira would have been lost without the GPS on her phone. Of course, she couldn't enter "super-secret CIA facility" into the directions app, but knowing where it was, she could scroll the map and plot her own course.

By the time they arrived at the facility, the sun had set. A pair of soldiers guarded the gate, as usual. When the truck stopped, they stepped out of the guard shack and approached from both sides. They wore desert fatigues with black tactical vests that read *Military Police* across the chest. Each man held an M4 automatic rifle on a sling over his shoulder.

"Uh...Samira?"

"Try to look like you're just a truck driver," Samira said. She rolled down the passenger window and showed them her badge.

"We weren't expecting a delivery," the guard on her side said. "What's in the truck?"

"The truck's empty," she said. "Hunt has some things he wants shipped out before the facility shuts down."

The other guard tapped on the driver's side window, and her dad rolled it down. "Identification please?"

He looked at Samira. "Give him your driver's license," she said.

He fished his license out of his wallet and handed it to the guard. The guard took it and walked back to the guard shack, where he picked up a phone. He looked at one side of the license, then the other, and spoke into the phone.

"Please stay in your seats," the guard on Samira's side said. "I have to check the back."

They heard the rear door open on its tracks. Samira's heart thudded in her chest like she had just sprinted the two hundred.

"What did you get me into here?" her dad hissed. "I wasn't planning on illegal entry of any government facilities today."

She did feel guilty about roping him into this. "It'll be fine," she said, hoping it was true. "Hunt's the facility commander, and he did give me permission for this. Sort of."

"Sort of?"

"Well, he more turned a blind eye. He implied that he wouldn't try to stop me."

"Samira…"

Samira knew her father wasn't above defying the government for a good cause. He and Mom had broken laws in Ethiopia on at least a dozen occasions, when it was a matter of protecting people's lives. She just hoped he would keep trusting her that this was one of those times.

They heard the rear door bang shut. The guard in the shack got off the phone and pushed a button that caused the gate to swing open. He returned to the truck and handed the driver's license back through the window. "The facility is closing, you said?"

"Yeah, didn't they tell you?" Samira asked. "It's because of the virus. They're shutting everything down."

"They never tell us anything," the guard said. "You're clear to go."

Samira and her dad raised the windows and drove on. After a while, her dad asked, "Where is it?"

"Right there, in front of us."

"That little building?"

"It goes twelve stories underground."

PAULA MET them at the door. "It's about time," she said. "At midnight, everything locks down."

"Why didn't he leave us with access all night?"

"He's covering his butt. He wants deniability. If things change at midnight, he can just say he was giving employees time to get their papers in order before they're archived."

Samira's dad cleared his throat.

"Oh, I'm sorry!" Samira said. "I guess you've never met. Paula, this is my dad. Dad, this is Dr. Paula Shapiro, my dissertation advisor and the best avian anatomist this side of the Atlantic."

"I've heard about you," her dad said. "You're the one who brought back the dodo."

"That's right," Paula said. "Lewis. He's our pride and joy."

"So did you get everything ready?" Samira asked.

"As much as I could. You'd better get down there, though. Alex has been talking to him, but he's pretty jittery right now. He needs you."

"Let's get down there, then."

The cavernous eighth floor echoed strangely with no one there. They walked past the lab tables and equipment, left in place as if to continue work again tomorrow. They took the elevator down to the twelfth floor. None of them bothered with the hazmat suits. They were way past that now.

They reached Charlie's living area. On the other side of the glass, Charlie stood on a low wooden perch and plucked at his neck feathers. Samira was shocked at the change in him. He looked thinner, his feathers had lost some of their color, and in places she could see raw skin where feathers should be.

"What happened to him?" she asked.

"He's just been sitting there, mostly, since you left," Alex said. "He doesn't eat and he doesn't talk."

Samira remembered the last conversation she'd had with Charlie, when she'd told him there just might be another one of his kind alive, but that he would probably never see it or know for sure. And then she'd abandoned him. She'd holed up in her apartment with Beth, leaving him alone. Of course he was despondent. She cursed herself for not even thinking about the effect that news would have on him. She probably thought of him as a person more than anyone else, but even she could forget so easily.

"That looks like a bird," her dad said. "I thought you said a dinosaur." He stood between Paula and Alex in his flannel shirt and ball cap, horribly out of place. He was a visitor from a different world, as surprising in this context as a polar bear in a rainforest.

"All birds are dinosaurs," Samira said. "But he's actually not a bird. He's an extinct, non-avian maniraptoran. Well, I guess not extinct, exactly. But his species has been gone for a long time."

"You brought him back? Like the dodo?"

"Actually, no. Charlie—"

"Let's get this show on the road before somebody stops us," Alex said. "Explanations can come later. Samira, you'd better get in there and tell Charlie what's going on."

"You didn't tell him?"

"I tried. I don't think he understood me. He doesn't want to talk to me, anyway."

"All right."

Alex pressed the buttons to unlock the outer door and the inner door leading into the cage, and she went in. Charlie didn't look up or acknowledge her presence. It was both frightening and exhilarating to actually be inside the cage with him after all this time. She could reach out and touch him if she wanted.

"I'm sorry I haven't come to see you," she said.

Charlie cleared his throat. She didn't know if he was actually clearing his airway, or if he had just learned to mimic the sound as something humans did before speech. "Sorry, sorry," he said in his strained, squawking voice.

"Do you know what's going on?"

"They hurt, take smell, hurt others," he said.

"I'm not going to let that happen."

"Let me die," Charlie said. The directness of it took her breath away.

Samira took a step closer, hands out. "I want you to live," she said. "I need you to live. You're important to me." She felt a rising sense of panic. Charlie had been through some horrible experiences. He should have died with the rest of his species, but here he was. How could she talk to him? She wasn't a psychologist. She wouldn't know how to give effective counseling to a grieving human being, never mind a dinosaur. "I need your help," she tried. "Humans are going to go extinct, too, if we can't stop it. All of us, dead, just like you."

That prompted the first flicker of interest. Charlie raised his head slightly and fixed one eye on her. "Asteroid comes?"

"No. This time it's a virus."

"Virus?" he tried, mangling the word. "What is?"

"It's...um. A disease. A sickness. It's spreading from person to person."

"Samira is sick?"

"No, not yet. But many humans are. It's spreading."

Alex rapped on the window. "Come on," he said. "We need to go."

"We're here to rescue you," Samira said. "To take you away from here, so they can't hurt you or use you to hurt others. Please come. Don't you want to see the stars again before you die?"

Charlie straightened and gazed at her directly. "Millions of years. Stars are different."

"Yes," she said, delighted that he knew that. "Come and see."

CHAPTER TWENTY-THREE

The freight elevator was enormous, like a two-car garage. It made sense for it to be big, since all the building materials to create the floors below had come up and down in that elevator. It could probably lift a tank. It also went straight to the surface, which was what they wanted.

They all filed in: Samira, her dad, Paula, Alex, and Charlie. It seemed insanely wrong and yet totally right at the same time for Charlie to be standing there with them, out of his cage. His head was just about at her height, and looking at his mouth full of teeth, Samira felt caught between an irrational terror that he was about to eat them and amazement that she was doing something as mundane as riding an elevator with what was essentially an alien species.

The elevator mechanism whirred to life and with a metal clank started hauling them toward the surface. Charlie tensed at the sudden sound and motion, his eyes going wide. "It's okay," Samira said, wanting to stroke his feathers but holding back. "It's taking us out."

The huge doors rolled open to a cool breeze and almost complete darkness. They stepped out, and Samira looked up.

The stars out here were brilliant. She could see the light pollution from Denver as a glow to the east, but besides that, the darkness was complete enough that the stars appeared in their thousands, with the rest of the Milky Way's two billion stars as a glowing splash stretching from the south to the northeast. Charlie crouched and cocked his head upward to see.

The elevator doors slid shut behind them.

"Well, isn't this a touching sight?" a voice said from the darkness.

Samira whirled toward the sound of the voice just as a pair of headlights blazed on, blinding them.

"Samira doesn't surprise me," the voice said, "but Dr. Shapiro? I thought better of you. I thought you at least had more sense.'"

Paula crossed her arms. "Is that you, Bowman?"

Sergeant Bowman, the muscular soldier who had endured cattle prod jabs to the stomach, stepped into the light, followed by three men in fatigues, all of them pointing M4s. The men were in silhouette, the headlights at their backs.

"Did Everson put you up to this?" Paula asked.

"He warned us you might try something. He requested additional security in case you did."

"You always did like to suck up to the boss," Alex said. "What are you getting out of this, a promotion?"

"This isn't about me," Bowman said. "You don't know me at all, so don't pretend you do. This is about you stealing classified government property."

Samira took a step forward, despite the guns. "He's not property. He's a person, just like you and me."

"I'm sorry about this," Bowman said. "But I'm not the villain here. No more talk. You're going to take that thing back downstairs and lock it up again. Now."

Samira was about to retort, but then closed her mouth, afraid of what Bowman might think of her. But that wasn't right—she didn't care what Bowman thought. Did she? She had to do what he said, though, there was no question about that. The gig was up. There was no point trying to resist.

"Come on, Charlie," she said. It was only as she turned back toward the elevator that she caught a faint smell, like sweet gasoline, and recognized it for what it was. Bowman was dominating them. The thought made her furious, but her anger quickly died when she considered the situation. He had the upper hand. There was nothing they could do. She knew it was the chemical making her feel that way, but that just made it seem all the more inevitable. What was the point in resisting?

The others turned back toward the elevator as well, meekly obeying Bowman's command. Samira's father shook his head, probably regretting his offer to help. Alex pressed the code that would reopen the elevator door. Paula whispered something to Charlie, presumably urging him to return with them.

But Charlie wasn't going. He stood his ground. He stretched his neck high and fluffed out his feathers. Suddenly, Bowman didn't seem like the powerful one. Samira no longer felt any need to obey him. Instead, in a primal impulse like a cross between fear and awe, she cowered before Charlie. He seemed to swell in size and strength, a beautiful and lethal demigod that could grant joy to those who followed him and death to those who rebelled.

"Run away," Charlie said to Bowman and his men, and even the squawk of his voice sounded majestic.

But the men did not run away. They stepped forward, and in the reflected light, Samira could now see the gas masks they wore. The one in front raised his rifle to his shoulder.

"Shoot it," Bowman said.

The soldier sighted in on Charlie and fired.

PREY DIDN'T RECOGNIZE the metal contraptions the men carried, but he recognized their pitiful attempts to dominate him with their scent. It was the first time any human had tried to communicate through smell, but they did so clumsily, like a child. He had expected to dominate them easily, but they ignored his command. "Shoot it," the leader said. Before Prey even understood what was happening, another man raised his metal machine and it erupted in noise and blinding light.

He didn't know what it was, and so he didn't know it could throw death. Paula knew, though. Paula, who had cared for him every day since he'd woken in the strange cage, even before he'd met Samira, started moving as soon as the leader spoke. She threw herself in front of him, holding up her hands and shouting for them to stop.

She was too late. As light and noise roared out of the machine, her body danced in front of him. Blood leaped from sudden wounds. Prey didn't know how, but he could tell it was killing her. A sudden searing pain in his shoulder told him that if she hadn't jumped in the way, it would be killing him instead.

Before Paula's body even hit the ground, Prey reacted. He was an analyst, not an athlete, but his legs were built for jumping and his body for killing. He leaped, not at the one firing his weapon, but at another one of the weapon carriers. The humans had to build weapons because they were prey animals, with no claws and tiny teeth useful only for chewing, not killing. Prey didn't need weapons. His powerful rear claws drove the man to the ground, and a quick snap of his jaws finished him. Prey's momentum carried him forward and he killed the second man before he even raised his metal machine. The man who had killed Paula whirled, his weapon raised, but Prey was faster. The light and noise flew wide, and Prey's teeth took the man in the throat.

The fourth man, the leader, carried no weapon. He

collapsed to his knees, staring wide-eyed at Prey. "Call him off!" he pleaded. "Don't let him hurt me."

Prey took a quick step forward. The man pulled something from his coat, something black and metal, but small. "Watch out!" Samira shouted. It was another weapon like the others. The man lifted it in his direction, but Prey lunged and took the weapon along with the man's arm. His scream died when Prey removed his throat.

The other humans rushed to Paula's side. Samira cried and held Paula's hand and stroked her hair. Samira's father held his daughter close, while Alex bellowed and held his hands to the sides of his head in anguish.

Prey licked the blood from his mouth. His instincts told him to eat the food he had just killed, but he knew that would be wrong. These humans looked and smelled like food, and he had killed them as thoughtlessly as if they were animals. But they weren't animals. They were people. He had killed count-less times in his life, but never people.

Samira looked up at him. He saw the wariness in her posture and wondered what she thought of him now. Would she want him dead, too, now that she saw the threat he posed?

"We've got to go now," Alex said. "This was an operation. Whoever told them to do this will know it went badly. We have to get out of here before they send more soldiers."

"We can't just leave her," Samira said.

"We can. We have to, if you want Charlie to live. She'll be found with the others."

Prey didn't know enough human language to say the things he wanted to say. Instead, he spoke in the way he knew best. *Be still*, he sent. *Grief can wait.*

He saw the effect of his words on them. Muscles relaxed, faces calmed.

Over the messages of calm acceptance, he sent a sense of urgency and speed. *We must flee. There is no time to waste.*

Samira stood. He was inexperienced at reading human

facial expressions, but her bearing communicated determination. "Let's get to the truck, then," she said.

She stepped around Paula's body, then paused. "Hang on," she said. She unclipped a thin, rectangular object from a braided rope around Paula's neck. The flat rectangle had her picture on it, as well as her blood. Samira wiped the blood off on the sleeve of Paula's cardigan. "I'm sorry," she said, and then louder: "Okay. Let's go."

Her father led the way to what looked like a large white box on wheels. Prey loped along behind them, prompting the humans to glance uneasily over their shoulders. Once again, Prey sent calm.

"Alex, you ride in the cab," Samira said. "I'll ride in the back with Charlie."

"No," her father said. "There's nowhere to sit back there. There's room in the cab, behind the seats. A little cramped, but you'll be safer than in the back."

"I'll be fine. I want to ride with Charlie."

"There aren't any windows. It'll be dark."

"All the more reason. He's been kept in a cage ever since he woke up. I want him to understand that he's safe with us. Or at least that we're on his side."

Prey didn't understand all the words, but he knew she was arguing on his behalf. He helped her out by sending a renewed sense of urgency.

"All right," her father said. "Just get him in there, quick."

Samira pulled a latch, and one side of the box lifted and curled up inside through some clever mechanical device. The inside of the box was bare metal. His eyes had grown accustomed to the starlight, but the box was dark and barely large enough to stand up in.

"You have to get inside," Samira said.

Despite the urgency, the thought of climbing into that box and having it close behind him filled him with fear. He couldn't step forward. He wished Meat or Distant Rain were there to soothe him. He could make the proper scents and inhale them himself, but it just didn't have the same effect.

Samira reached out and clasped his hand. The move startled him. The fleshy softness of her fingers repelled him at first, but besides the texture, their hands were not all that different. She had a tiny, useless-looking finger where she should have a second thumb, but the idea of a hand, the muscles and the joints, were the same. She pulled on him, and he realized she was leading him forward into the box. He let himself be led.

The box had thick straps attached to the wall. "These are for cargo, but we'd better strap in so we don't slide around back here," she said. Sitting on the floor, she wrapped one around her own waist and clipped it to a hook on the wall. He couldn't sit like her, but he crouched and clipped a strap around himself as he'd seen her do.

Samira's father pulled the door closed, plunging them into darkness. Prey could see a faint rectangle where the door had been, but aside from that, nothing. He couldn't even see Samira.

"Hold on," she said.

A roar vibrated through the box, and Prey thought: Is it alive? All of the human machines he had seen so far had been dead, made of metal and wood and other unrecognizable materials. This 'truck' as they had called it rumbled like a growling beast and then started to move.

Prey scrabbled for purchase on the slick floor, his claws scraping with a hideous shrieking sound. He knew he smelled like fear, but he couldn't help it. This was so unexpected and so far outside his experience that he couldn't help reevaluating. Did the humans mean him harm? But no, Samira was right here with him.

"It's all right," she said. "It's a truck. We're slow creatures, so we need machines to help us get around."

Get around what? Prey didn't understand, but he was too

afraid to try to ask. Human words took such effort and thought to produce, and his mind had fractured with fright.

The vibrating increased, and the truck rocked and lurched. His mind fled into another place and time. The ground bucked beneath his feet. Hot air stung his eyes and made it hard to breathe. A fireball tore across the sky, and the whole Earth seemed to break apart with nowhere to escape. Prey couldn't breathe. He shrieked his terror, which only echoed in the metal box and pummeled his ears. Finally, through the din, he heard Samira shouting his name.

"Charlie!"

It wasn't his name, not really, but it was what Samira called him. He didn't know how to translate 'Sweet Blood of Easy Prey Just After Slaughter' into her language, and he didn't know what 'Charlie' meant, so he couldn't express it in his own.

"It's okay," she said. "You're safe. It's okay."

She was right. He was unharmed. The noise of the truck had settled into a low hum, and the jouncing wasn't as bad as before. There was no immediate danger.

But she was wrong, too. It wasn't okay. His entire species had died in the disaster he had just been reliving. He didn't know how to process that, or if he ever could. But it would never be okay.

His breathing slowed. The noise of the truck became mesmerizing. He might almost have fallen asleep, if not for the emotions crashing through his mind. His species, gone. The taste of human flesh on his tongue. His utterly alien surroundings. He didn't belong here. He wanted to go home. But home didn't exist anymore.

Samira and the others were risking their lives, and for what? Wouldn't it have been better if he had just died with the rest of his race? There was nothing for him here but danger and sorrow and eventually, death.

"You controlled us back there, didn't you?" Samira asked.

Prey tried to mimic the unfamiliar word with the extra lilt at the end that made it a question. "Controlled?"

"You manipulated us," she said. Another word he didn't understand. "You made us leave Paula. You forced us." He smelled the bitterness on her, the salt of her tears. She was suffering, too.

"Forced you leave, no," he said.

"I smelled it. You were manipulating us. Making us react how you wanted us to."

He hadn't forced anyone to do anything. "No forced," he said. "Talking."

"Talking? You didn't say a word. You just pumped those pheromones at us and made us leave her body behind."

Prey considered. How could he make her understand? It was so difficult speaking her language, especially to talk about emotion. Emotions were chemicals. How could anyone communicate emotion with only sound?

"No forced," he said again. "Alex say we go. You say we stay. Talking only. I talk too, my way. No push or fight. Just talk. Make feel better. Say we go fast."

"Your way of talking packs a bit more punch," she said.

Prey snarled in frustration, not understanding again. Did she get what he was saying or not?

"I'm sorry," she said. "I understand, or I think I do. You were just trying to convince us. But you do it too well. You don't leave us a choice."

CHAPTER TWENTY-FOUR

S amira could barely feel her legs anymore, and every muscle in her back ached. Anger boiled in her gut without relief. Anger at Charlie, anger at Bowman and his eagerness to pull the trigger, anger at Paula for being dead, anger at herself for leaving Paula behind. Halfway through the trip, she started banging her fists on the metal flooring just to feel the pain.

At that moment, she almost wanted God to exist so she could rage at him for making such a messed up world, where whole species could die at the gravitational whim of an orbiting pile of rock or a scrap of protein with a talent for replicating itself. She needed there to be a reason. If God had killed Paula, it would have been part of some grand, unfolding plan, and she could have hated him for that. But without God, there was just no reason at all. She needed to know why, but there was no why. The question itself had no meaning.

Samira wished she could have planned this rescue better. With no time to prepare, she hadn't thought much further than getting him out of the facility. If she was honest with herself, she hadn't expected to get this far. They had succeeded in getting him out. Now what?

It was one thing to spring a dinosaur from a secure government lab; it was quite another to keep him secret with the government on their trail. Where could they possibly hide him? It's not like she could take him to her apartment. Ideally, she would have found some empty field or woods to hide in with a lot of land and no visitors, but she didn't have anything like that. She had to go with what she knew, and what Samira knew was the University of Colorado Ornithology Center.

The truck stopped moving and the engine died. They had arrived.

The door rolled open and Dad and Alex helped her climb down. It was still night, but the streetlights and the light from the nearby stadium meant it wasn't very dark. This was the riskiest part, with the most danger of being seen. The streets of college towns were rarely empty, even in the middle of the night, but at the moment the threat of the Julian virus was keeping more people inside.

They crept toward the building, a ridiculously conspicuous sight: three people leading a living dinosaur through a college campus. There were cameras, but she wasn't too worried about those. No one would look at the recordings unless there was a break-in or some other reported crime, and if someone knew enough to report a crime, it would already be too late.

They saw no one. So far, so good.

Samira used Paula's ID card to open the door. They were headed for the development lab, where Lewis the Dodo had been hatched and hand-raised. The lab was off-limits to all but a very few: those who had good reason to be there and knew enough not to risk damage to fragile biological specimens. Lewis had enjoyed a habitat inside the lab before being moved to his current home, with both indoor and outdoor accommodations. As far as Samira knew, his old habitat was currently empty, and what was better, inaccessible to most people. It was the only place she knew where Charlie might, just possibly, stay safe and secret, at least for a day or two, until they could figure out a better option.

They crept through empty and dark hallways, Charlie's claws clicking on the hard flooring. She wondered what sorts of floors Charlie's people had used, if they had constructed floors at all. Soft, mossy coverings, perhaps, that claws could grip without destroying? Or horizontal ladders, with no floors at all? They passed the avian center, where Marcy the raven and Mikey the cockatoo were probably sleeping.

At the lab, Samira pressed Paula's card against the reader. The light turned green, and a whirring sound in the door-frame accompanied the release of electromagnetic locks. She turned the handle, and the door swung open.

The lab was split into two areas, much like the underground lab that had housed Charlie. Half of the space was behind glass—the habitat where Lewis had been raised—and the other half was designed for the human scientists. As soon as she saw it, Samira began to doubt the wisdom of this plan.

If Paula had been with them, this could have worked. Paula knew how to update the system to control who had access to the room, and the authority to pull it off. She would have been able to bring in supplies without suspicion, at least for a time. How could they do it without her? Samira didn't even know who could get in here, or when they might suddenly appear.

She didn't even want to keep Charlie a secret, not really. She wanted to show him to the world. But how could she do that now? As soon as the CIA knew where they were, they would swoop in and clean up the mess. Even if they could stay hidden somehow, they might not control the narrative. Everson could publish pictures of the soldiers Charlie had killed and spin up public fears of rampaging dinosaurs. If he blamed her and Paula as reckless scientists and painted it as a *Jurassic Park* scenario, they could kill Charlie—or even just pretend to kill him—and the public probably wouldn't even object.

Samira closed the door behind them. They would be safe here for the night, at least. They could get a little sleep and figure out what to do in the morning.

A sudden clatter and a loud curse from the opposite end of the room drove her heart into her throat. She looked in that direction, but all she saw was a counter with several microscopes on top of it. Then something moved underneath. A young man rolled off of a cot hidden in the shadows and clambered to his feet. He was tall and terribly thin, and he swept unruly hair out of his eyes to stare at Charlie. "Whoa," he said. "You have got to be kidding me."

Samira hunted in her memory for a name and came up with it. "Trevor," she said. He was the graduate student who'd been working in the avian lab when Samira had picked up Wallace after returning from Thailand. She cursed herself. It should have occurred to her that someone might be here even this late at night. She'd slept over at the lab more than once herself as a student working long hours.

"That's a dinosaur," Trevor said with certainty and awe. "A maniraptor, am I right?" He finally tore his eyes away and looked at Samira. "Was this Paula's big secret project? That she's been disappearing off to so much?"

Samira sighed. "Yeah."

"Wow. This is incredible. How did you get the DNA? What surrogate did you use, an ostrich? What method did you use to introduce the genome into the germ cells? Where's Paula?"

Samira felt a lump forming in her throat and pushed past it to speak. She remembered how much she'd loved Paula as a graduate student, and doubted Trevor felt any different. "I've got bad news," she said.

She told him, and he cried. She didn't know this kid at all, but she felt a surge of affection for him as he tried to hide the tears that ran unbidden down his face. She sat with him, a hand on his shoulder, while Alex took stock of the room, opening all the drawers and cabinets and examining the equipment.

"We're going to need some food for Charlie pretty soon," Alex said. "Did you have a plan for that?"

Samira looked up. "Me? This is Paula's place. She might have had a plan, but not me."

"He needs live prey, not just meat. Where are we going to get that?"

"I don't know! We'll figure it out."

Alex's eyes were wide. "Figure it out? We're not going to last here. How long do you think we can keep this a secret? As soon as it gets out that Paula is dead, people will be coming through here to check on her projects. Someone else will take over her job. And how do you propose we bring live animals in here without anyone noticing?"

"We're not going to figure it out by panicking," Samira said. "We're all in shock and grieving for Paula. We need to get what rest we can and—"

She stopped when her father lurched forward, holding both hands over his mouth.

"Dad? Are you all right?"

He lurched again, and this time his hands came away and he couldn't hold it back. He vomited bright red blood on the floor.

SAMIRA FELT WEAK, like her legs might suddenly give way. She tried to think of reasons why her father might be vomiting blood. Maybe he had a stomach ulcer. Or a tear in his stomach lining. But she knew it wasn't any of those things. He was infected with the Julian virus.

She rushed forward to help him, but Alex grabbed her around the waist and held her back.

"Stay away," her dad said, his voice a painful croak. "You know what this is. You can't help me by catching it yourselves."

Trevor, looking terrified, leaned carefully forward and passed him a roll of paper towels.

"You should all stay here," Dad said, wiping his face. "I'll make my way to a hospital."

"Wait," Samira said. "What about Mom? Is she sick? Is that why she didn't come with you?"

"No," he said miserably. "I mean, I don't know. I didn't know *I* was sick. She was really tired, which is unusual for her."

Samira thumbed the icon on her phone to place a call to Mom, but it rang with no answer. She tried Beth next, who answered right away. "Samira? Where are you? Where have you been?"

"Look, there's a lot to explain, but the most important part is, Mom may be sick. She's at home, but she won't answer her phone."

"Sick...as in…"

"Yeah."

"Did you try Dad's phone?"

"Dad's here with me. At the university." Samira didn't want to tell her, but that wasn't fair to her. "Beth, he just threw up blood."

"Oh no!"

"I'm afraid Mom may be sick, too, but no one is with her. You're closer, and I know there's a quarantine, but—"

"There's no more quarantine. I'm on my way."

"What?"

"They lifted the quarantine. This thing is just every-where now, and Denver's not even the worst. They need the Army more in other places, and the line in the sand they drew here is meaningless. They announced it a few hours ago."

"So you're going to go check on Mom, then?"

She heard a car door slam. "Already on my way."

"I'LL TAKE you to the hospital," Samira said.

Her dad shook his head. "That's stupid. You'll only get infected yourself. I can still drive." He lurched to his feet, a little unsteady, but walking fine. He took a few steps toward the door. It all seemed so logical: you get sick, you go to the hospital. As if he had any hope of coming back again.

"Wait!" Samira cried. Her eyes stung and her chest hurt. "Don't go. They're overrun at the hospital; there won't be any free beds. And if this really is Julian, they won't be able to help you."

"If I stay here, I'll just get all of you sick," he said. "If I haven't already."

"Then stay in there." Samira pointed to the glass enclosure where Lewis had spent the beginning of his life. It was just an empty space now, but it would keep him separated. "And if it isn't Julian, then you'll get better."

Dad's flat smile told her what he thought of that possibility, but he nodded his head. "Okay," he said. He didn't want to walk away and never see her again either.

"Take the chair with you," she said. "And here—take Trevor's cot."

"Wait, what?" Trevor said.

"Come on, he's sick. He'll need to lie down."

Grudgingly, Trevor pulled the cot out from under the counter and handed it over. Dad took it and the chair and dragged them through the glass door into the enclosure. He shut the door behind him. It clicked with a sound like the end of the world.

THEY STOOD THERE, staring at each other in horror, nobody knowing what to say, until Charlie moved, scraping one claw against the floor. Samira jumped and realized that for the first time, she had actually forgotten there was a dinosaur in the room.

"What is happening?" Charlie asked in his harsh voice.

Samira suddenly felt bone tired. "The sickness I told you about," she said. "Many humans are dying." She pointed into the enclosure. "Now my father is sick."

"I help," Charlie said.

"Help? How?"

"Change. Not sick."

"I don't understand."

"Change." She could see he was frustrated, not having the words to express what he was trying to say.

A pungent smell filled the room. *No*, Samira thought. *We don't have time for memories.* Too late, she felt herself sliding into another time and place.

PREY STOOD *at the edge of a modification pit, fifteen days before impact. He could see his reflection in the dark liquid, rippling gently in the granite ravine below. Could this actually work? Could they actually survive here?*

Distant Rain joined him at the edge. Through all their work together, she'd been teaching him more than he'd ever understood about how this technology had developed. He knew the liquid had been invented to store scent communication, so that the stories of his people could be remembered and passed down, but he hadn't known much more than that.

She'd taught him how the power their bodies naturally had to synthesize scent had given them dominance over their prey and formed the basis for their social hierarchy. Obvious, perhaps, but it had never occurred to him to connect their way their bodies worked to how their society was structured. Scent, she taught him, was also chemistry. Chemicals that could strip organic material down to its basic instructions, that could sample it, alter it, and coax it to replicate in new patterns. They'd learned to build complex chemicals that operated like machines. Once that was possible, those machines could be combined into larger and even more complex chemicals, and those larger machines into chemicals that represented whole systems of interaction and change.

Eventually, they learned to tailor plants and animals—and males— to best fit the jobs they were needed for. No one person could remember how to make chemicals of such great complexity, though, so that knowledge was stored in the pits, where those trained in their use could inhale them, read them, and apply them to the task at hand.

"It's going to be hard for some of the females to accept," Prey said. "The idea that they might have to be modified too."

Rain bobbed in agreement. "They think they're what's keeping our species pure. That if we modify everyone, we won't be people anymore. We'll start a genetic slide that causes us to lose our true nature."

"But isn't that true?" Prey asked.

Rain snorted. "Not hardly. Or I should say, it is true, but it's not new. Our species has been sliding for thousands of years."

"Male modifications are enough to have a noticeable effect?"

"Sure, eventually. But it hasn't always been just males, either, despite what our current leaders would have you believe. Females have been modified, too. In fact, our whole species has been modified en masse, and more than once."

They walked around the edge of the pit, watching as cranes raised a wooden platform dripping with liquid.

"A hundred years ago, there was a skin disease that ravaged the coastal roosts and spread westward. It was both disfiguring and dangerous, leaving sufferers susceptible to infection and killing many. The modification engineers found a way to alter us to resist it. I suspect there have been more, too, forgotten over time, or intentionally buried. The greater size and strength of the females—was that given them by evolution? Or was it *modified intentionally to give them power? Maybe a thousand years ago, it was males who dominated society."*

That didn't sound likely to Prey—in nature, the whole purpose of life was reproduction, and it was females who did the reproducing. They could choose which males to accept, and thus whose genes would be passed on to the next generation. It only stood to reason that they would have the most power.

Distant Rain brought him inside, where a rush of conflicting smells made him cough. "It takes some getting used to," she said.

Rows of organic blanks stood to the side, waiting to be programmed into walking load carriers, memory storage devices, bioluminescent light fixtures, music players, egg creches, nest cleaners, and a wide array of living entertainments and toys. But none of those things were being created now. Instead, the blanks were being used to test the modification fluid. Dozens of them had been shaped into eerie facsimiles of Rain herself, in different stages of transformation.

Prey shuddered as she showed them off with evident pride. "They look just like you. How can you stand to look at them?"

"They're not really alive," she said. "Well, technically alive, but not thinking or feeling. And the modifications are working well. Which is good, because we don't have much time left to redesign."

Prey walked down the row of subjects, trying to imagine those changes happening to him. If all went well, he would be finding out what it was like quite soon. It didn't seem real.

"The whole world is going to change," he said. "Our whole species, if we survive."

Distant Rain came up behind him. "There's one more story," she said. "A myth really, from before we learned to store memories and pass knowledge reliably from generation to generation."

"Before civilization, then," Prey said.

"Not exactly. We believe there was civilization even before we learned to store memories, and some technology, too, but knowledge could only be passed directly from individual to individual. We have no record of it, only stories told across the years. But according to those stories, we first developed the ability to manipulate the chemistry and genetics

of our own body to combat a disease. Legend says a plague swept through the world that was so bad it threatened to wipe out our whole species."

"The Death Scent," Prey said. "But that's just a story, isn't it? A tale for children."

"I'm not so sure. I think the plague was real, and we adapted ourselves to survive it. Or maybe it was the plague itself that first made us who we are, genetically altering survivors to be able to understand our own body chemistry through our sense of smell."

Prey shook his feathers. "That seems unlikely. Diseases exist to make copies of themselves, not to provide new skills to their hosts."

"My point is, however it happened, this isn't the first time we've changed ourselves dramatically to meet an extinction threat," Distant Rain said. "We'll get through this, and we'll still be us. A thousand years from now, they might not even remember what we did, but our species will still be here."

Prey looked at the last organic blank of Distant Rain. It was heavier than the real Rain, with an extra layer of fat and a thicker coat of feathers. Its teeth had been altered to allow it to eat a wider variety of food, and he knew its digestive system had been similarly changed. It didn't look much like the Distant Rain he knew. "I hope you're right," he said.

WHEN SHE CAME to herself again, Samira started to tell Alex, but Charlie's scent had reached both of them, and he had seen the same vision.

"Why did you show us that?" she asked Charlie. "Are you telling us there might be a way to cure him?"

"Yes. Might."

"Meaning you could engineer a drug? One that could cure anyone who has the virus?"

"Might." Charlie approached the spot on the floor where Dad had thrown up blood. He ducked his head and circled, sniffing it. "I need pit."

Samira glanced at Alex, then back at Charlie. "You want us to dig you a pit?"

"No. Real pit. Made by my people. With chemical tools in."

"But those pits are in Thailand," Samira said. "They're on the other side of the world. Not to mention that it's been millions of years. Can't you do it without that?"

"You go my home and my time and build truck? With none of tools?"

"No, I guess not. But Thailand—"

"Might not even then," Charlie said. "I not know much. Not like Rain."

"Wait a minute," Alex said. "Where's Trevor?"

Samira looked around. She'd been caught up in the vision, and she hadn't been paying attention to the young intern.

"He's gone," Alex said. "This is bad."

Samira gripped the back of her neck and groaned. "He's going to tell someone. I don't blame him for panicking, but what are the chances he's going to keep this quiet? Even forgetting about Charlie, we've got someone with the Julian virus in here. He might have been exposed. He probably called 911 the second he stepped out the door."

"And they probably notified the military's virus hotline. Which means the CIA might already know where we are."

"We have to go. Now." Samira yanked open the door to the glass enclosure. Her dad looked up in surprise. "Change of plans," she said. "We're running again."

THEY HEARD the sirens as soon as they burst through the doors. A group of college students on the other side of the street—five white boys with virtually identical T-shirts, fraternity ball caps, and bottles of beer—gaped at the sudden appearance of a dinosaur.

"Whoa. Check this out," one said. He strutted across the street with the others close behind.

"In the truck," Samira said. "Ignore them."

The fraternity boys blocked her way. "Hey, baby, slow down. What is that thing? Is that yours?"

"Out of our way," Samira said, but they didn't hear her. They had frozen, their eyes wide. She caught a familiar whiff of petroleum. For her, the smell brought no terror, just a feeling of deep loyalty to Charlie. For the fraternity boys, it was a different story. They shook where they stood, and a dark wet patch appeared on the front of the leader's pants. Charlie lunged in their direction, snapping his teeth, and they fell to the ground, groveling and crying.

He stalked past them toward the truck, and Samira followed, impressed but also a little horrified at Charlie's display. What would become of the world when all its petty leaders and bullies had that kind of power?

The frat boys would remember seeing a dinosaur, and would tell others. They were at least somewhat drunk, so they might not be believed by most, but the CIA would believe them. Even if Trevor kept his mouth shut about Charlie, they would know he'd been here. How could they possibly hope to hide a dinosaur? Anywhere they went, *someone* would see them, and word would get out.

Someone would see them. An idea started to form in her mind as they ran for the truck and clambered aboard. Dad insisted on riding in the back with Charlie this time, so Samira took the passenger seat. As Alex gunned the engine and headed away from the sound of sirens, the idea grew in her mind. It was crazy, and possibly catastrophic, but they were beyond caution. And it just might solve all of their problems at once.

She dragged her phone out of her pocket and dialed Kit's number again. He answered on the first ring.

"Kit, it's me," she said. "I need some help."

CHAPTER TWENTY-FIVE

They raced westward toward the mountains, with Alex at the wheel and Dad and Charlie hidden in the back of the truck. The peaks and cliffs of the Rockies shone with the light of the sun rising behind them, as glorious and aloof as every other morning. The mountains had stood tall before there were humans, and maybe would still after humans were gone.

Alex had a pass in his wallet for Rocky Mountain National Park, so they decided their best route would be over Trail Ridge Road, straight through the mountains. They drove through Estes Park, and the road started to climb steeply, hugging the sides of the mountains in sweeping switchbacks. To their left, steep rocky cliffs rose toward the sky, while on their right, the ground dropped away to distant valleys and gorgeous vistas.

Samira called Beth before she lost phone service. "Beth? Did you find Mom?"

"I'm here with her now. She's fine. Seems like she just had a cold or something. No signs of Julian, though she's pretty worried about Dad. Are you still at the university?"

"No. We're on the run." Time to come clean. "We rescued Charlie, Beth. We got him out of there."

"Oh, Sami."

"We had to. They were going to hurt him, probably kill him before long. I couldn't just do nothing. And Beth…" She could hardly get the words out. "They shot Paula. Bowman and his goons. They killed her." She choked up, and tears spilled down her face.

"No. Oh no. Samira, where are you? How can we get to you?"

"I can't tell you. They're after us. They're probably listening in."

"Is Dad still with you?"

"Yes. Okay, listen. You remember Pinky and the Brain?"

A pause, then Beth said, "Yes."

"Not the cartoon. The joke. You remember?"

"Are you talking about—"

"Don't say it. Not on the phone. That's where we're going. The place where we told that joke. Can you meet us there?"

"I guess."

It was the best option Samira could think of. "Pinky and the Brain" had been a ridiculous and short-lived nickname for Arun and Gabby, awarded late one night at an ichthyosaurus dig site, when Arun had been sunburned and Gabby couldn't stop going on about what sunburn did to the body. No one else but the two of them and Beth could possibly know the joke, or where they had been when they'd made it.

"We'll meet you there," Samira said. "Don't tell anyone where you're going. Leave your phone where you are. Mom's too. I'm going to get rid of mine, so you won't be able to contact us. Just meet us there, okay? And try to make sure you aren't followed."

"You're scaring me, Samira."

"That's because I'm scared."

A beat of silence from the other end, then: "Okay. We're coming."

"Good. I love you, Beth."

"When we get there, you'd better tell me the whole story."

"I will. Everything. I promise."

Samira called Gabby and gave her the same cryptic message. After hanging up, she used Google Maps to look up the route to Tijuana, Mexico. She studied it carefully, took note of the major turns. It was a long way, but it just might work.

She flipped her phone over, but there was no way to take the battery out, and she wasn't convinced that just shutting it down would stop it from being tracked. She rolled down the window. She drew back her arm and sighed. This phone had cost her $500. Oh well. She flung her arm forward and let go. The phone arced out over the gap and disappeared, falling out of sight to the rocks far below.

"What are you doing?" Alex asked.

A big curve in the road ahead featured a parking lot with bathrooms and coin-operated binocular stations to look down into the valley and at the mountains on the other side. "Pull over," she said.

"I thought we were in a hurry."

"I think they can track our phones. We have to get rid of them. Dad's too."

He parked so the back could be opened without any tourists getting a look inside. She opened it long enough to explain the problem to Dad and get his phone. Then she threw it off the edge.

"You next," she told Alex.

"How can I navigate to where we're going without my phone?" he complained.

"Hang on a sec." Samira rummaged in the truck and came up with a pen and an old receipt. She wrote down the directions, looking them up on his phone to double-check.

Then she handed the phone back to Alex. "Your turn," she said.

Reluctantly, he drew back his arm and let it fly. It glittered in the sunlight as it fell.

Back in the truck, they continued their ascent. Great walls of snow rose to their left, evidence of the massive drifts that had covered the road before the huge plowing machines dug their way through. Finally, they came over a rise, and a whole new range of mountains rose into view, snow caps striking up at the clear blue sky.

"We've reached the Continental Divide," Alex said. "It's all downhill from here."

Samira nodded. "Only nineteen hours of driving to go."

DAN EVERSON ARRIVED at the ornithology lab with six soldiers and an FBI forensics expert. The police had already been through, and so the crime scene—if it could be called one—had already been examined by the locals. They'd found paper towels with bloody vomit in the trash can, some traces of the same on the floor, a cot, sleeping bag, and pillow, and a lot of scientific equipment that had likely been there already.

They also had Trevor Cameron, who was either playing dumb or was the most dimwitted kid ever to attend college. He talked like a surfer on marijuana, and seemed to forget more than he remembered about the things Alex, Samira, and her father had discussed when hiding in the lab.

"Did they want something here?" Everson pressed. "Were they here to get something they needed, or just to hide?"

Trevor swept hair out of his face. "I don't know, man. They just came in, and then the old guy was like, ugh, right on the floor, and I was like, I'm getting out of here."

Everson rolled his eyes. He was dominating the kid, so he

was pretty confident he was telling all he knew. "Did they say anything about where they were going?"

"Dude, there was a frickin' *dinosaur* in the room. I wasn't paying attention."

Everson's assistant, Michelle, pushed through the doors. "I got the university to give us access to Paula's staff voicemail," she said. "Listen to this." She picked up a phone in the lab, pressed a button, listened, waited, and then pressed another one. She pressed the speakerphone button, and an accented voice sprang out of the phone's speaker into the room. "Dr. Shapiro, we received the picture you sent of the product you have available for sale. As you suggested, we are interested in owning a matching set. We will meet you at the location you indicated in two days' time and arrange for transportation from the harbor there. We will guarantee you safe passage and payment in full upon delivery."

After the message finished playing, Everson said, "No way she made that contact in the last twelve hours."

"You think Paula and Samira have been working for China all along?" Michelle asked.

"It's possible," he said, though he didn't really think so. Samira might not be as patriotic an American as he could have asked for, but she called too much attention to herself to be a spy. Unless she was far more talented than he'd given her credit for.

"I had the call traced," Michelle said. "It originated in Dusit Palace in Bangkok."

"Thailand," Everson said, rubbing his chin. Like the rest of Southeast Asia, it was rapidly turning into a Chinese protectorate. Had Paula and Samira really been willing to hand over the most powerful weapon of the war to their enemy? If China gained enough power to seriously contest the United States, there could be a real shooting war, with millions dead. She would risk that to save a dinosaur?

"What harbor could they be headed for?" Michelle asked. "Surely not in the US."

"No," Everson said. "I can't imagine how they would pull that off. There are dozens up and down the coast, but they're all crowded places with constant traffic. They could put him in a shipping container, I guess, but they'd need a lot of help to make that happen secretly. Too many checks, too many people involved."

"Mexico, then?"

"That's more likely. US Border Patrol is a lot more interested in trucks coming into the country than going out. A Chinese ship could take on mystery cargo there with fewer checks and fewer questions."

"I'll contact Border Patrol and alert them to be on the lookout."

"Might not help if they can dominate their way through," Everson said, sighing.

This whole thing was a disaster. Somehow Bowman and his team had managed to shoot Paula, though how that had happened he would never know, since the dinosaur had torn them apart shortly afterward. He was angry at Samira, and even angrier at Paula, who he thought would have known better than to pull something this foolish. There was no way this was going to end well.

"She's headed for China, one way or the other," he said. "We have to stop her."

"What if we can't?" Michelle asked.

"It'll be up to the Director at that point, or maybe the President, but I think we either intercept this delivery, or we put special forces on the ground in Yunnan Province. I can't emphasize the severity of this enough. If we lose this creature, we lose the war."

SAMIRA RODE with her cheek resting on her hand, staring out the window at the darkness. At first, she and Alex had managed some conversation: the virus, the likelihood of their escape plan working, the resources of the people chasing them. After the first few hours, however, the conversation ebbed, and she was left with her own thoughts.

What was happening in the back of the truck? She imagined her father jostling around back there, getting sicker and sicker. She would gladly have given him her seat, or he could have used the little bench in the cab behind the seats, but he had insisted on the back, presumably so that he wouldn't spread the disease to them. Could he spread it to Charlie? The disease crossed species lines, after all. But the memory Charlie had shown her implied that his species might be immune.

Maybe she should have left her dad at the university. When the police came, they would take him to a hospital and see that he was cared for. But as her dad had pointed out, they couldn't really help him at the hospital either. They couldn't heal the disease, and they were so overwhelmed with patients they probably couldn't even help with the symptoms much, either. Even so, she felt horrible about shutting him in a dark box for hours on end without so much as a bed or a seat. She tried not to imagine opening it and finding him dead.

Her mind flashed back to the image of Paula lunging forward just as the guns began to fire. She saw her body spasm as bullets punched into her, saw bloody wounds appear as if by magic. The images repeated on an endless loop, obscuring the dim scenery outside. In her mind, she screamed every time, even though she wasn't sure she had screamed at all when it had actually happened.

In fact, she couldn't remember what she'd done. It hadn't even occurred to her to throw herself in the line of fire. Who did that? Who could possibly make the decision to die for someone else so quickly that they could get there in front of the bullets? No hesitation. The reaction of a moment, and then she was dead, with no way even to know if her sacrifice had been worth it.

Would she, Samira, give her life for someone else? For Beth, for instance, or one of her parents? She'd like to think she might, but when it came down to it, could she really go through with it? To be snuffed out, forever. What could possibly be worth that?

She didn't realize she was clenching her fists until she felt her fingernails digging into her palms. With an effort, she relaxed her hands. She hated to be helpless. She wanted to *do* something, to *fix* it, but no one could ever fix Paula again. She was gone, and it was wrong, and there was nothing at all Samira could do about it.

The best she could do was to make her death count for something. Paula had died to save Charlie, so Samira would make sure Charlie survived. She would make sure Charlie lived long enough to save everyone else.

A few hours after sunrise, they stopped at a convenience store in Beaver, Nevada, between a post office and a Mormon meetinghouse. It was a drab, flat town with dirt lots and stunted trees, and the convenience store had the same prefab aluminum look as the rows of trailers behind it. The town's only saving grace was that the flat and treeless landscape gave an unobstructed view to the Rockies in the distance. The Mormon church parking lot was empty at this time on a weekday morning, so Alex parked there, facing the back of the Isuzu toward a dirt field containing nothing but a few abandoned propane tanks, a shed, and beyond that, some railroad tracks.

Samira opened the rear door, her muscles jittering with fear, terrified she would find her father lying on the floor of the container, dead or almost so. Instead, he jumped out almost as soon as she opened the door.

"Wow, it's good to get out of there," he said. He stretched his arms over his head, then looked at her. "What?"

"You gave me a heart attack! I thought I'd find you on the floor."

"Nope. I'm feeling a lot better. The time passed quickly, in fact. Charlie's been telling me—or showing me, I guess—his memories of his life, and I've been telling him about Jesus."

"Wait," Samira said. "You've been *evangelizing* the dinosaur?"

Her father shrugged. "We were just talking. They have a concept of God in his culture, but not a personal one, not someone you could know or talk to. He does understand the idea of sin and evil, though, so I was telling him how Jesus—"

"Enough, I get it. I'm glad you're doing so much better." She looked at Charlie. "Did you...heal him?"

Charlie nosed his way to the open door and stuck his head out, breathing deeply of the fresh air. His claws scraped on the corrugated metal floor of the container. "Not heal. Slow sickness only. He feeling better, but not for always."

"What do you mean?" Dad said. "You made me feel better? How?"

"While he was showing you his memories, he was sifting through the chemicals in your body," Alex said. "He's got that amazing sense of smell, and then the ability to produce tailored chemicals of his own. He's like a walking pharmaceutical research lab."

"That's amazing," Dad said. "Could he do that for others? We should bottle whatever chemical he's using and send it to the hospitals."

Samira shook her head. "That's what we just rescued him from. Other people using him as a drug synthesis machine."

"But if he can help people survive this disease?"

"First of all, he's standing right here," Samira said, growing angry. "He can understand you just fine. So if you want to convince him of something, talk to him, not me."

"I'm sorry, I just—"

"Second, we're trying to get him to a place where if he's

willing, he might not only be able to heal the symptoms for a few people, but mass produce a cure that could reach the whole world. But first we have to get him away from the people who want him to be a weapon. Understand?"

"Got it," Dad said.

Samira looked around, making sure no one could see the dinosaur poking its snout out of the back of their truck. She went into the store and gathered an armful of trail mix, protein bars, and bottles of water. At the last moment, she remembered to pay with cash instead of her credit card. At some point, money was going to turn into a problem.

Back outside, she saw Alex coming out of the post office, and frowned. What had he been doing in there? "Ready to go?" he asked.

"One more thing," she told him. "I have a call to make." She pointed at the side of the convenience store, where a payphone stood.

"There are still places with payphones?" Alex asked. "You've got to be kidding me."

"Time moves slower in a town like this," Samira said.

She dug a few quarters out of the Isuzu's cupholder and walked over to the battered phone. She lifted the black receiver, slid a quarter into the slot, and dialed one of the numbers she'd written down earlier. A tinny ring sounded from the plastic earpiece, which was already making her ear sweat.

"Hello, this is Evelyn."

"Dr. Soderberg?"

"Yes."

"This is Samira Shannon."

"Yes, Dr. Shannon! I've been trying to reach you. Your tip about the horseshoe crabs was an excellent one. They moved heaven and earth to get me some a few hours after I asked, and they do appear to be immune, as you predicted. The infected ones and the uninfected ones seem equally healthy."

"So you believe me. That this virus is from the Permian."

"It seems a likely possibility, though not at all one I'm pleased about. It's going to be a long road to crack this one. We've never seen anything like it."

"What if I told you I have someone who has not only successfully slowed the progress of the disease in a patient's body, but has a pharmaceutical lab that may have the capability to cure it altogether."

"It sounds like a miracle, if it's true," Soderberg said. "Who are we talking about? What lab?"

"I can't tell you that," she said. "There are problems. Political problems."

Silence from the other end. Then: "What can you tell me?"

"I'm on the run from the government. The science that might give us the cure? They wanted to use it as a weapon. I got out and took it with me."

"And the person you're talking about, the scientist or doctor who's had some success attacking the virus; he or she is with you?"

"It's more complicated than that, but essentially, yes. He's with me."

"And this lab you're talking about? Where is that?"

Samira sighed. "I can't tell you."

"I see." A pause. "And what do you want from me?"

"I want you to come with us."

"And you can't tell me where?"

"Not unless you're coming. I can't risk it. But I hope you'll agree to come. We have a chance to beat this thing, and if we have an infectious disease specialist with us, I think our chances will be better."

"What about your miracle-working scientist?"

"He's not exactly a scientist. He's...well, you'll see."

"You can't tell me."

"No."

"But you want me to drop everything, all the work I'm trying to do here to find a cure, and run off to join you in a dangerous and probably illegal venture in an undisclosed location, based on the word of a person I've never met and only spoken to on the phone twice."

"I understand," Samira said. "It was a pretty big ask, but I had to try. I hope you find a cure there; I really do."

"I'll be honest with you," Soderberg said. "It's not going well. The more we spin our wheels, the more all of the frightened government officials around us interfere in the process. We're working eighteen-hour days, but the biggest break we've had is the immunity of the horseshoe crabs. Which, I don't have to point out, came from you."

"I'm glad it was helpful."

"Look," Soderberg said. "I'm sure you have good reason for what you're doing. Stay in touch. If you have any lab results you can share, any more insights, anything at all, please let me know. Can I call you on your cell if I have questions?"

"I threw my phone off a cliff. So...no."

"You're not kidding, are you?"

"I'm afraid not."

"You're making me nervous, Dr. Shannon."

"You and me both."

CHAPTER TWENTY-SIX

They drove for hours across flat and sandy Nevada, the Rockies never seeming to get any smaller behind them.

"What was that letter you sent?" Samira asked.

Alex didn't look away from the road. "Letter?"

"Come on, you know what I mean. The letter you sent at the post office."

"It was a letter to my family. To let them know why they might not see me for a while." He glanced at her. "Don't worry, I didn't give any details. They'll be able to tell the post office it came from, but we'll be long gone by the time it gets there."

"Your family?" Samira asked. "You know, we've been working together all this time, and I don't think you've once mentioned them."

His expression didn't change, but his fists tightened on the steering wheel. "I have twin girls. They live with their mother. I have visitation rights on the weekends."

She could tell there was a lot of emotion and hurt behind those few sentences, but she didn't press. "I'm sorry," she said.

He let out a breath. "Don't be. She was right. I was all

about work, and I was never home for them. And here I am, doing it again."

"How old are they?"

"They're eight." He smiled. "Little princesses, the both of them."

"You're making the world safe for them," she said.

"I hope so."

THREE BLACK SUVS skidded to a halt in front of the Beaver, Nevada post office. Everson stepped out, scanning the surroundings for danger. Not that he expected any. The fleeing scientists had stopped here briefly, at least according to one Kenny Buck, who worked in the Beaver post office and had reported two quarantine runaways that matched the description of Samira and Alex to the virus hotline. The Denver quarantine had been lifted, but Kenny apparently didn't know that. He'd been regularly reporting any strangers who showed up in town coming from that direction.

The sun shone brightly in a cloudless sky. Everson felt a trickle of sweat run down from his temple. He didn't understand why anyone lived here, in this nothing town with no trees and no attractions and nothing to recommend it but the postcard-perfect view of the Rockies in the distance. A town like this, everyone knew your name and everything about you. Everson hated that feeling.

"They stocked up on food," a soldier said, coming out of the convenience store. "No security cameras, but Mr. Buck confirmed there was a Black woman with them, and I get the idea that's pretty rare around here."

"Just food?" Everson asked. "No weapons?"

"Nah. They sell some ammunition in there, but no guns. All they bought was food."

Michelle came out of the post office holding a letter.

"What's this?" Everson asked.

"This is why they went into the post office. Alex sent a letter to his family."

"Open it."

Michelle shook her head and handed the letter to Everson. "Federal crime."

"And I'm a federal officer." He took a K-Bar from its sheath at his side, sliced the envelope open, and pulled out the single, handwritten sheet.

Madison and Avery,

I know it's been a while since I visited. Too long. Your mom takes care of you better than I ever could, but that's no excuse. Remember the last time I was there, when we painted the garage together? I still have some paint under my fingernails. I miss you terribly, but I'm sending this to tell you that I'm not going to be able to make it for your birthdays. In fact, I'm not sure when I'll be able to come again. I got in some trouble, and there are people looking for me. I'm going to have to go away for a while, and I don't know when I can come back. I know I'm doing the right thing, and if I could tell you what I'm doing, I think you would be proud of me. My one regret is not being able to see the two of you.

Give love to your mom,
Alex

EVERSON GRUNTED and slipped the note back into its envelope. He handed it to Michelle.

"Anything good?"

"Just that they're leaving and not planning to come back. But we already knew that."

"What should I do with it?" she asked.

He nodded toward the post office. "Get our friend Mr. Buck to put some kind of "damaged in transit" sticker on it, drop it in a larger envelope, and send it on to Alex's family."

Another soldier rolled down the window of his SUV and said, "Sir, you're going to want to hear this."

Everson ducked inside, back into air-conditioned comfort. The interior of the vehicle looked more like a tactical command unit than a suburban family car, with reconnaissance and communications equipment installed in the dashboard and weapons racks in the back. The soldier pushed a few buttons, and a woman's voice with a Hispanic accent came over the speaker system.

"*Kit! Wow, how have you been?*"

"What am I listening to?" Everson asked.

The soldier paused the recording. "This is Gabriela Benitez, one of Samira Shannon's known associates. We've been tapping her phone. You remember we heard Samira call Gabriela late last night, right after she called her sister, Bethany."

"Yes, all that nonsense with Pinky and the Brain."

"Right. Some kind of rudimentary code that we couldn't decipher, probably based on shared experience. We just got a break on that."

The soldier restarted the recording.

"*It's so good to hear from you,*" Gabriela's voice said. "*We didn't even get to say goodbye.*"

"*It's been a crazy time,*" a man's voice replied.

"We've identified that as Dr. Chongsuttanamanee, a Thai paleontologist from Samira's team," the soldier said.

"*Did Samira tell you the plan?*" Gabriela asked.

"*Yes. That's why I'm calling, though. I can't reach Samira.*"

"*She threw away her phone. She's afraid they could track her with it.*"

"*Right. The problem is, I don't have the specifics on where to meet up with her. Tijuana's a big place. She said you'd know, something about an old cartoon called Pinky and the Brain?*"

Gabriela laughed. "*Yeah, we went to the beach down there, and Arun didn't think he needed sunscreen, and I wouldn't let him hear the end of it.*"

"*Okay. What beach?*"

"*It's south of the major tourist beaches, called Playa del Rosarito. There's no harbor to speak of, but Samira said you'd be able to get a small boat right down to the sand.*"

"*Well, not me personally, but yeah, they can do that. She said Thursday at noon. If I can't contact her, though, how can I know she's on schedule?*"

"*Just have to trust her, I guess,*" Gabriela said.

Everson smiled. Samira thought she was so smart. Always questioning the importance of his methods, chafing against the rules, arguing for openness and transparency. Now here she was, with a textbook case of sloppy operational security leading to complete intelligence failure. Samira, at least, had thrown away her phone and used simple coded references, but without disciplined security by her entire team, the information had leaked.

Tijuana. Playa del Rosarito. Thursday at noon.

With that information and the direction they'd traveled so far, he would stop her for sure, maybe even before she reached the border.

"Three ports of entry to get across to Mexico," he said. "San Ysidro is the most likely, but let's get people to all three. Much easier if we intercept them before they leave the country. Contact the customs authorities there with the license and description of their vehicle. I assume you've provided that to California Highway Patrol as well?"

"It's done," the soldier said. "They're mobilizing a thick presence on southbound Routes 5 and 15 from LA to San Diego. They know to detain but not to look inside the truck."

"Hopefully we'll catch up to them before they get that far," Everson said. "Let's roll out."

SAMIRA AND ALEX raced southwest through Nevada, heading toward California and the still-distant Mexican border. Samira, taking her turn behind the wheel, was starting to doubt the wisdom of this plan. At one point, a police cruiser blazed past them, sirens wailing, and she thought they were finished. She felt exposed on the barren highway, without so much as a tree to hide behind. She kept imagining she heard the chop of helicopter rotors following them from the sky.

Finally, she pulled to the side of the road across the street from a community of dusty mobile homes.

"What are you doing?" Alex asked.

Samira pointed off to their left. "Elk. He hasn't eaten since the lab."

"Shouldn't we get farther south first?"

"I don't know when we'll get another chance. And the farther south we go, the bigger the risk."

"Okay. He'll have to be fast, though."

He was fast. Two dozen elk watched, unperturbed, as Charlie ran through the grasses toward them. Dominated by his scent, they didn't move even as he struck the smallest and tore out its throat. He ate his fill quickly, then trotted back to the truck.

By that time, a small crowd had formed in front of the

mobile homes, shielding their eyes from the sun and looking incredulously at the dinosaur climbing back into the truck.

"Mission accomplished," Alex said. "Let's get out of here."

"WE'RE GETTING SOME CHATTER," Michelle said. She was working the SUV's comm equipment from the passenger seat, a pair of headphones over her ears. "Multiple calls from a trailer park outside Twin Falls, Nevada, reporting a velociraptor or a giant bird-monster hunting and killing elk out on the plateau."

"Did it escape?" Everson asked. "Is the thing running loose now?"

Michelle put a hand to one ear, cocking her head to listen to the headphones. "Doesn't sound like it. They reported it being loaded into a truck. Local law enforcement sounds skeptical. Don't think they're responding very quickly."

"Get them moving," Everson said. "Contact police in the next several towns south, too. We've got them boxed in now. Nowhere to run."

SAMIRA STEPPED ON THE GAS, pushing the truck as fast as she dared. Those people from the mobile home community were going to start telling people what they saw. She didn't think any of them had been close enough to get a credible photo from a phone, but the story might make the news anyway. Everson would know they'd been there soon, if he didn't know already.

The truck rattled and bounced alarmingly, but she didn't let up. If they blew a tire, they'd be done for, but she had to risk it. This was the critical part of the trip. Either they would make it, or they'd be caught. The only thing she could do now was drive.

EVERSON JUMPED out of the helicopter behind the police barricade, three hours' drive south of the mobile home community where Samira and the dinosaur had been spotted. Only an hour had passed since the first photos had hit social media: blurry, low-resolution shots from a distance of a large creature feeding on an elk. There was no way they could have gotten past this point already, no matter how fast they were driving. They could take other roads, of course, but he had checkpoints posted on all of those as well, and the border authorities on high alert, just in case they somehow slipped past. Everyone had been warned that this was a biological terrorism threat and likely Julian virus infection: do not approach, do not investigate the vehicle, do not allow suspects to get close. Just hold them until the professionals arrive.

Nothing to do now but wait. Everson sat on the hood of his black SUV until it got too hot, then retreated into the air conditioning inside. An hour passed. Two.

He slapped the dashboard. "Where is she? Any word?"

Michelle shook her head. "Nothing yet. They're in an old truck. Probably doesn't move very fast, and they might have stopped for gas or food."

They waited some more. He was starting to worry that they'd missed something when Michelle sat up straight and pulled her headphones off of one ear. "Highway patrol thinks they've spotted them. Five miles out, coming our way. They're following behind to cut off their retreat."

"Good," Everson said, his adrenaline spiking. "Tell them no lights, no sirens, and stay back. If they turn around, block the road but don't engage."

"They know," Michelle said.

"Tell them again!" The last thing they needed was a bunch of armed policemen dominated into shooting each other.

Michelle spoke into her microphone. Everson climbed out of the car and back into the heat. He jogged toward the row of police cruisers who were stopping and checking each vehicle that came through. A long line of cars reached out beyond the checkpoint.

"Let them all through," Everson shouted. He reached the first cop and lowered his voice. "The terrorists have been spotted. We need to get this line clear."

The cops sprang into action, waving the cars through. The line slowly shortened as the traffic passed through without stopping. Eventually, it cleared, and Everson was looking at an empty stretch of road. He found the highway patrol officer in charge, a bulky man with a ridiculous waxed mustache.

"Where are they?" Everson demanded.

"Any moment now."

A white spot appeared in the distance, then resolved out of the dust into a boxy white truck. Finally. The truck slowed, but made no move to turn around. Everson expected them to pull a U-turn once they saw the barricade, or even accelerate to ramming speed, but the truck slowed gently and approached with caution. Maybe they planned to dominate the cops. He didn't actually know if that was possible without a lab to refine the scent chemical, but he wouldn't put it past Samira and Alex to figure it out.

The sergeant raised a megaphone and bellowed for the vehicle to stop. Cops fanned out and raised their weapons. The spinning LED lights from the police cruisers reflected off of the truck's windshield, preventing a view inside the cab. Everson felt a sick feeling in his gut. His intuition told him something was wrong.

"Step out of the truck with your hands up," the sergeant shouted.

A bearded, heavyset man with blue overalls and thinning hair stepped out of the truck, his hands up and his eyes wide as saucers. Everson had only seen Samira's father in a photograph, but this didn't look like the same man.

"Get him clear and check the truck," Everson snarled at the sergeant.

He turned back to the SUV. He already knew it wasn't them. Where had they gone?

He hurled the door open, climbed in, and slammed it closed again. "Any other sightings? Anything from the other roadblocks?"

Michelle looked at him in surprise. "It's not them?"

He shook his head, then punched the dashboard in disgust. How was this possible? A bunch of amateurs with no training, driving a *dinosaur* through California, and yet he couldn't track them down? They must have had help. He'd assumed the Chinese contact was merely for pick up in Tijuana, but they must have someone in-country, a professional spy who was helping them evade capture.

He knew they weren't coming now. They waited at the blockade for several more hours anyway, but no dinosaur-carrying truck appeared. Samira Shannon had somehow slipped the net.

CHAPTER TWENTY-SEVEN

Samira's muscles slowly relaxed as they drove north, each mile bringing them farther away from the careful breadcrumbs they'd left for Everson and the CIA to follow. There was no way to know if it had worked. Maybe he wasn't even tapping their phones. But she thought he probably was.

The 'Pinky and the Brain' incident had not occurred in Tijuana, as Gabby and Kit had intentionally staged their conversation to let on. It had happened on a ranch near the Oregon badlands where Samira, Beth, Arun, and Gabby had worked uncovering an ichthyosaurus one summer back in her graduate student days. The dig site had been on ranch land owned by a paleontology enthusiast by the name of Brook Waters, who had welcomed their team eagerly and since become a patron of their work. That was where the team was headed; not to Thailand or China or Mexico.

They had intentionally staged the elk hunt, too, making sure Charlie was seen, to leave evidence confirming that they were headed south. With any luck, the CIA had believed their misdirection and would be looking for them a thousand miles away from their actual destination.

WHEN THEY CROSSED INTO OREGON, the only indication was a small wooden sign on the side of the road. The barren wilderness went on for miles in every direction under a stark and cloudless sky. Not exactly the lush greenery of Charlie's home, but they would take what they could get.

Three hours later, the view had barely changed. They pulled into Waters Ranch, named for the five generations of Waters sons who had raised cattle there rather than any natural rivers or lakes. In the distance, Samira could see the green of pasture and the latticework of metal irrigation pipes that kept it that way. Everything else for miles around was flat and brown. A few hundred cattle milled listlessly inside a wooden pen.

Now was the moment of truth. Samira hadn't been able to think of a way to contact Brook ahead of time, not if she wanted to keep their destination a secret. She was about to show up on his doorstep with a dinosaur wanted by the CIA and hope he would welcome them.

She stopped the truck and climbed out. As the dust drifted away, she saw Brook in the distance, wearing jeans and a broad-brimmed hat and heading their direction. She couldn't really make out his expression, but he walked with what looked like wary concern. She doubted he had many unexpected visitors in unfamiliar vehicles, and that when he did, it was rarely a good thing.

"Open the back," she told Alex. "Get everyone out."

"Even Charlie?"

"Especially Charlie."

When Brook came close enough that she could make out his craggy, weathered face, she called out to him. She put her hand up, half in greeting and half to shade her eyes from the setting sun.

"Samira?" he said. "Heavens, girl, what are you doing here?"

"I'm sorry," she said. "I would have called if I could."

He reached her and wrapped his arms around her. "Been a long time," he said. "You never write."

"Sorry," she said again. "You know how it is."

"What's going on? Who are your friends?"

With a little help from Alex, Samira's father stepped down from the tailgate. He looked remarkably good for someone riding in the back of a truck for hours, never mind for someone with a deadly illness. She realized again how much she was asking of Brook—not just to harbor them from the government, but to invite the Julian virus right to his doorstep.

"That's my dad, and my friend Alex," she said. "But the last one in the truck will take a little more explanation…"

At that moment, Charlie sprang from the truck. He landed gracefully, talons splayed and toothy mouth agape. His protofeathers stuck out all over his body, making him look larger than he actually was.

"Whoa!" Brook stumbled backward several steps. In moments, though, he recovered himself and stared. "Samira? Is that what I think it is?"

"That depends. Do you think it's a theropod dinosaur alive and well in Oregon?"

"I can't believe it." He took one step forward, circling slightly as if approaching a frightened animal. "I've been following the news, but I didn't even know you guys were *trying* to bring back a dinosaur. I didn't think it was possible with animals that old."

"It's not, generally speaking. This is kind of a special case. Brook, meet Charlie."

"Hello," said Charlie in his squawking voice. "Glad meet friend."

Samira laughed as Brook's eyes seemed to bulge out of his head.

"We've got a lot of explaining to do," she said.

THE REST of the team joined them at the ranch, all except Kit. Gabby and Arun arrived first, and Samira had to tell the stories all over again, and then yet again once Beth arrived with Mom.

When the car pulled up, Beth jumped out with a shout and ran to her for a hug, her head only barely reaching Samira's collarbone. Mom was even faster, catching Dad up into an embrace and then holding him at arm's length to study him, her face drawn with stress and her eyes red with tears. "Samira said you were sick."

"I was. I am. I still have the virus, but Charlie slowed the symptoms. You shouldn't get too close."

"You idiot," she said, burst into tears, and hugged him all the harder. Finally, she looked up at him. "Who's Charlie?"

BETH BROUGHT A SURPRISE WITH HER, too. She returned to the car, ducked into the back window and came out with a red-and-green macaw, a little bit windblown but otherwise none the worse for wear.

"Wallace!" Samira exclaimed. She reached out, offering Wallace her arm.

Wallace squawked indignantly and shuffle-stepped up Beth's shoulder, working his way around to the other side, away from Samira.

"Oh, I know," Samira said. "But I'm here now. You'll forgive me, won't you?"

Beth slipped Samira a package of peanut butter crackers, and once Samira offered him one, he grudgingly deigned to come to her.

Samira rubbed a finger against his feathers. "Mercenary bird. You're just in it for what you can get."

Later, they sat on porch chairs outside of Brook's house and watched Charlie run through the fields.

"Incredible to watch," Beth said. "I've been modeling his musculature for months, and this is the first time I've seen him really use it."

A steer stood grazing, unaware of the feathered engine of death approaching it from behind. Charlie didn't even have to dominate it; the steer never stood a chance. Charlie leaped. He landed with both feet and jaws striking it simultaneously and drove it to the ground. After one throaty bellow, the steer fell silent. Charlie sliced jaws through its flank, then yanked at an angle, tearing off a slice. He threw his head back like a heron swallowing a fish, and gulped the piece down whole.

"I'm sorry," Samira said to Brook. "This must be costing you a fortune."

"Are you kidding?" he said. "This is a sight not witnessed in sixty-six million years. Do you know how much people would pay to see this? I'm getting a bargain."

"I can't pay you," Samira persisted. "I'm basically asking you to harbor us as fugitives, at least until I can figure out something better. The CIA will be looking for us. If they find us—"

"Enough," Brook said. "Ever since you got here, you haven't stopped trying to convince me to kick you out. This is the most amazing thing that's happened to me since uncovering that ichthyosaurus on my back acres. Did you know I've been taking a paleobiology course online from the University of Alberta?"

"No. Seriously?"

"I have. Makes me want to sell the ranch and get my degree."

"Oh, you wouldn't do that, would you?"

Brook sighed. "No, not really. Not exactly practical, and

I'm too old. But don't try to convince me that having a real, live, intelligent, talking dinosaur eating my cattle isn't the best thing that ever happened to me."

Samira laughed. "Okay. But I don't promise not to feel guilty about it."

"I have almost a thousand acres for Charlie to hide in, a supply of food, room in my house for all of you to stay, and more money than I need. This is the perfect place for you to be."

"At least for a little while," Samira agreed.

DAN EVERSON CRUSHED his empty coffee cup and hurled it out the window. They'd been tricked. Samira Shannon, a naive amateur, had laid a false trail, and he'd blindly followed it. He'd let his disdain for her and poor security practices cloud his judgment. She could be anywhere in the Western United States by now, or in Canada, or halfway across the Pacific on a Chinese ship docked at some other harbor. There were dozens of small harbors up and down the coast with a lot less security than the big ports. She could even have doubled back to some farm in the Midwest.

Agents swarmed Playa del Rosarito and the other Tijuana beaches, but he already knew they would find nothing. Samira hadn't been seen crossing the border, despite guards looking out for her face and vehicle. Her father's truck hadn't been spotted by any highway patrol south of Salt Lake City. And now the other members of her dig team had gone missing, their phones off the grid and their vehicles unaccounted for. He kicked himself for not having agents assigned to them for surveillance, but before Samira's sudden flight with the dinosaur, he would have had no real reason to spend the manpower.

This had turned from a chase into a search. That meant

bringing in local law enforcement across the Western US in a massive bioterrorist manhunt. He'd check satellite imagery to see if he could track where they went, but he doubted he would find anything with sufficient resolution that happened to be looking at the right place at the right time.

In short, this disaster was about to turn into a huge expense for the agency and a huge black mark for him. Until this week, he'd been a star, central to one of the most important missions in the intelligence community. Now, if he failed to recover this dinosaur, it might cost him his career.

Which meant he absolutely would not fail. He still controlled the stores of chemical he had extracted from Charlie and processed at the black site in Colorado. He might not explicitly have authority to use them for this, but he hadn't explicitly been forbidden to, either. Somebody had to know something. If she wasn't leaving a money trail, it was because she was relying on friends. He would dominate every person she'd ever known, if necessary, to find out the truth.

And if she really did have help from Chinese infiltrators? If she'd already defected to China and left the country with the dinosaur? Then he would do everything in his power to get them back.

CHAPTER TWENTY-EIGHT

The stars stretched across the Oregon sky like a blanket of diamonds, with only a hint of light pollution glowing on the western horizon. Brook sat on the grass, leaning back against his hands and gazing up at the brilliance. Charlie lay on the ground like a bird, his taloned legs tucked under his body and invisible beneath his feathers. He rested his head in Brook's lap and gazed up at the bright heavens with him.

Samira smiled at the sight. Brook and Charlie had bonded in a matter of days, apparently undaunted by the genetic gulf between them. Brook had always treated his horses as if they were intelligent, speaking creatures, so it had seemed like nothing to him to accept Charlie as an equal and friend.

"That's Aquila the Eagle," Brook said, pointing at a constellation. "An eagle is a descendent of your kind, a powerful hunter. You might see one flying over the ranch sometime. To the left is Cygnus the Swan. That's another big bird, one that lives in the water and can migrate as much as four thousand miles."

Samira walked on, leaving them to it, and sat down with her mom by the embers of their dying campfire.

"How are you doing?" Samira asked.

"Oh, you know, hanging in there."

"I'm sorry for all this. Pulling you away from your home and friends, making you a fugitive. I know it's not what you signed up for."

Her mom lifted her chin. "I signed up to be your mother. That means loving and supporting you no matter what. I'd say this is exactly what I signed up for."

Samira leaned over and gave her a brief hug. "Thank you."

Her mom looked up at the stars. "I know God is working all of this toward some great purpose."

Samira sighed. "It would be nice to think so."

She looked up at the sky. As glorious as it appeared, she knew she was seeing only a paltry fraction of the hundred billion stars in the Milky Way, which was itself just one galaxy among hundreds of billions. So much unseen, so much that would never be known.

She glanced back over at Charlie, lying in Brook's lap while Brook stroked his feathers. Her mind boiled with questions to which she had no answers. What did their future hold? How long would they be able to hide here? What would happen to Charlie if the world discovered he existed? Was there any free life possible for a creature like him in a modern human world?

She couldn't see how there could be, but she hoped so. Whatever came later, they had this moment, free and safe in a patch of Earth's natural beauty. They would all just have to wait together to see what came next.

EPILOGUE

Distant Rain Sweeping Towards Home as Night Falls woke yet again in her bare, odorless cell, wishing she could die. Death wouldn't be that hard to accomplish. She knew how to use her own chemicals to alter her body. The changes she could make were limited—she couldn't, for example, turn into a snake and slide through a small hole to freedom. Changing her glands to produce a chemical that would kill her, though, that she could do. She would simply fall asleep and never wake up.

The alien creatures would be here again soon with their wire nooses and the sticks that delivered jolts of lightning from their tips. They would drive her back with shocks whether she fought or not, and snare her neck and legs with their nooses. They would force her down to the floor and harvest the chemicals from her scent glands. Chemicals that, when threatened, she instinctively tailored toward dominance and control.

She wanted to die, but she wasn't ready to kill herself, not yet. For one thing, she wanted to understand what had happened to her and to the world since she'd entered the hibernation liquid. For another, she didn't want to die until she had taken revenge.

. . .

THIS IS the end of Book 2 of the <u>Living Memory</u> series. Look for the conclusion to the series, *Memory Reborn*!

OTHER BOOKS BY DAVID WALTON

Living Memory

The Genius Plague (Winner of the Campbell Award for Best SF
Novel of the Year)

Three Laws Lethal (Wall Street Journal Best of SF List 2019)

Terminal Mind (Winner of the Philip K. Dick Award)

Superposition

Supersymmetry

ACKNOWLEDGMENTS

Much of this series takes place in Thailand, which I have visited, but not nearly long enough to really capture the culture and places described in the book. Thanks to "Woodstock" Roehrig, who actually lives there, for helping me get it right. Thanks as well to Nadim and Julia Nakhleh, whose sage critiques of plot and characters helped refine the book to its current form. Thanks to Alex Shvartsman for publishing advice and ebook formatting. Thanks to Dr. Michael Brett-Surman, formerly Museum Specialist for Dinosaurs, Fossil Reptiles, and Amphibians at the National Museum of Natural History of the Smithsonian Institution. This book has many flights of fancy which are not his fault, but he reviewed an earlier draft and helped me get the real paleontology right. Finally, thanks to you, dear reader, for taking a chance on this book when you had so many other options available. I hope you enjoyed it!

ABOUT THE AUTHOR

David Walton is an aerospace engineer and the father of eight children. His love for dinosaurs started as a boy, but it wasn't until his own young son's enthusiasm that he really started to learn about how they lived and what they were like. His research obsessions have also included fungus (*The Genius Plague*), self-driving cars (*Three Laws Lethal*), and quantum physics (*Superposition*). When he's not writing, he's reading, playing piano, watching dinosaurs through his binoculars, or laughing with his family around the dinner table.

CPSIA information can be obtained
at www.ICGtesting.com
Printed in the USA
LVHW040048210423
744936LV00004B/53